Below decks, [...] shackled to the b[...] port side and men to the starboard. The slaves-to-be were terrified and chanted prayers to their gods who, it seemed, had deserted them. The fumes from the urine and solid waste that rose from the open hatches was about as foul as any can get.

The first officer was exhausted from lack of sleep. It was his first crossing on a slaver and he didn't like the idea one bit. The chanting and wailing human cargo had kept him from getting a decent night's sleep since the ship pulled away from the Ivory Coast six days earlier.

"Chin!" the first officer shouted to the man standing guard at the forward hatch, "get down there and shut them up! I can't stand anymore of that damned hollering!"

Chin climbed through the open hatch into the stench below. He stood at the bottom of the stairway, waiting until his eyes adjusted to darkness.

An Archangel arrived and took a position on the stairs just behind him, where she rested invisibly in spite of being in full view of half of those chained below. Several milliseconds later, another but very different form, was at her side.

"What's so important that we had to meet here?" the Archangel asked.

"I? I want nothing. I have come to make you an offer."

"What kind of offer?"

"An offer to put an early end to these silly games we play."

"What do you propose?" She braced herself for another of his ridiculous suggestions.

"I propose we let ten generations of mankind determine its```` own fate. We'll see how many lives are lost by man's own hand and how many are saved. If more are lost, then I win and we shall have an immediate accounting of souls, rather than waiting any longer. Whoever deserves damnation will be mine and whoever doesn't will be yours."

"And if more lives shall have been saved at that time?"

"It is not possible, but if it should happen, there will be no claiming of souls and everything will continue as it has, except that I will allow mankind an additional ten thousand years before I claim what's mine."

* * *

Mary's reaction to Father O'Brien's proposal was immediate: "Never. I could never leave Baltimore. It's my home. Why would I go out West where there are savages, wild animals and smelly fur trappers?"

"There's a world that you can't even imagine out there. I've read that there are herds of over a million buffalo that quietly roam the plains and sunsets too beautiful to imagine." He was whispering as he stared at the picture he had created in his mind. "There are noble Indians who wear beautiful hats of feathers and the men are closer to the hand of God."

"It sounds as if you should go, Father, rather than I."

"My parish is here and I am too old to make such a journey. Besides, 'tis a wife John March needs, not a priest."

"I should travel thousands of miles," she asked, furrowing her brow, "to marry a man I've never laid eyes on?"

* * *

Sam was putting more wood on the fire and Mary was scrubbing their tin plates with handfuls of dirt when they heard a horse snort a short distance away. They both stopped what they were doing instantly and looked into the darkness beyond the firelight. The flickering flames sent rays of orange glow out into the darkness where it danced across the ground. Mary quit rubbing the tin plate she had been cleaning and stood up straight. Then she slowly moved closer to Sam.

In a few moments, Sam could just make out the image of a man on horseback. Slowly the image came closer, like a ghost approaching silently. The horse seemed to be walking on pillows, lifting its legs high and setting them down deliberately, easily.

Finally horse and rider were within the ring of firelight. It was an Indian straddling a spotted pony. He was a proud, but very young warrior of a small band that had broken ranks with the Shahaptian Tribe nine years before. The pony he rode was from a strong line that would be known as Appaloosa. The young warrior carried an obsidian pointed spear adorned with two brown and white mottled feathers. The Indian guided his mount to a position effectively blocking Sam's access to the wagon, to the rifle that lay under the wagon's worn oak seat.

* * *

This is for Donna

This is also for the critics. Without them we may stand taller, but we only stand still.

Acknowledgments

Many thanks go to Marilyn Pesola, first my editor, later my agent, and always a good friend. I needed her unflagging faith in the reading public, her skill with red ink and her love for the written word.

The Judgment Ring

Book One

The Chinook River Princess

by
Jack Duckworth

The Characters and events in this book are fictitious. Any similarity to real persons living, dead, or reincarnated is coincidental and not intended by the author.

Be advised that this story's setting is not historically accurate; not even close. It is a story for the sake of entertainment and should not be mistaken for literature.

Published by Judgment Ring Books, a wholly owned subsidiary of Expert Systems Programs and Consulting, Inc.

The Chinook River Princess

Copyright © 2000 by Jack Duckworth

All rights reserved. No part of this book may be used or reproduced in any manner whatsoever without written permission except in the case of brief quotations embodied in critical articles or reviews, and in part or whole by the Columbia Lighthouse for the Blind for the use of the sight challenged. For information address Judgment Ring Books, 9501 Tinker Court, Burke, Virginia 22015-4155

ISBN 0-9679119-1-5   First Printed Edition

Printed in the United States of America

Chinook River Princess Audio CD Edition
ISBN 0-9679119-0-7   February 26, 2000

Prologue

The Origin of the Judgment Ring

The deck planking groaned and squeaked as the schooner cleaved the blue-black waves of salt water. The sky was clear except for a few high wispy clouds. The wind was from the Southeast at twenty-five knots and it kept the ship heeling about ten degrees to starboard. The captain was in his cabin, plotting a course for Savanna, Georgia, and the first officer was at the helm.

Below decks, one hundred and ten blacks were shackled to the bulkheads. Women were chained to the port side and men to the starboard. The slaves-to-be were terrified and chanted prayers to their gods who, it seemed, had deserted them. The fumes from the urine and solid waste that rose from the open hatches was about as foul as any can get.

The first officer was exhausted from lack of sleep. It was his first crossing on a slaver and he didn't like the idea one bit. The chanting and wailing human cargo had kept him from getting a decent night's sleep since the ship pulled away from the Ivory Coast six days earlier.

"Chin!" the first officer shouted to the man standing guard at the forward hatch, "get down there and shut them up! I can't stand anymore of that damned hollering!"

Chin was not much more than a slave himself. The captain had bought Chin three years before, when he put into Shanghai after an outbreak of a contagious disease had cost him over half his crew. Chin had worked sweeping floors and doing the laundry for a whore and opium house in Shanghai—until he fell in love with one of the women. When the owner of the house discovered him sampling the wares, he had Chin gagged, bound, and taken to C.H. Woo, his brother-in-law who was a merchant on the docks. Woo sold Chin to the Captain for the equivalent of ten dollars. At first Chin was livid, but in time he adjusted to ship's life and learned to love life on the sea. He found the open expanse of the ocean a welcome relief from the overcrowded humanity of Shanghai.

Chin climbed through the open hatch into the stench below. He stood at the bottom of the stairway, waiting until his eyes adjusted to the darkness.

An Archangel arrived and took a position on the stairs just behind him, where she rested invisibly in spite of being in full view of half of those chained below. Several milliseconds later, another but very different form, was at her side.

"What's so important that we had to meet here?" the Archangel asked.

"I thought you might like to see the results of your latest and most grandiose experiment." The scaly ugly creature tilted back his oversized, horned head and let out a throaty laugh.

"Why do you choose to appear in such a disgusting form?" Her distaste was apparent.

"I choose to appear as ugly as the human heart is treacherous—the human heart
that rejected your Father's flesh offering. Nothing is so ugly as rejection and they surely rejected Him." He sneered and swept his arm in a grand gesture across the sea of tormented black faces, "just as they reject these poor souls. His brothers and sisters stretched him on a timber rood to suffer, die, and putrefy in the hot sun. Admit it—you resent every one of them!"

"I resent none of them," she responded with quiet conviction. "I understand their weakness, as did he."

"Weakness, ha! They're strong and getting stronger, bad and getting worse. Mankind is basically evil and in the end I will have my share."

"Mankind is basically good and loving and in the end, all will be returning to the Creator."

"We shall see," he challenged.

Almost as if on cue, Chin yelled to be heard above the chanting and singing, "Damn you! Shut up!" His words were in Chinese, but it wouldn't have mattered if they had been in English, Spanish, French, or any other major tongue because the blacks understood only their own narrow dialect. Chin pulled a long-blade knife from the scabbard on his belt and waved it menacingly at the small knot of blacks in the stern who were chanting and slapping their chests in an anguished prayer for salvation.

"Why did you want to meet? What is it you want?" the radiant angel asked.

"I? I want nothing. I have come to make you an offer."

"What kind of offer?"

"An offer to put an early end to these silly games we play."

"What do you propose?" She braced herself for another of his ridiculous suggestions.

"I propose we let ten generations of mankind determine its own fate. We'll see how many lives are lost by man's own hand and how many are saved. If more are lost, then I win and we shall have an immediate accounting of souls, rather than waiting any longer. Whoever deserves damnation will be mine and whoever doesn't will be yours."

"And if more lives shall have been saved at that time?"

"It is not possible, but if it should happen, there will be no claiming of souls and everything will continue as it has, except that I will allow mankind an additional ten thousand years before I claim what's mine."

"Ten generations is an awfully short time to determine the fate of mankind. What's ten generations in our Father's time?"

"Your Father, not mine!" The frustration and anger shone clearly in the dark angel's words. "To Him it is but an instant, to me an eternity. I'm bored with watching and waiting. I want the souls that I am due and I want them soon."

Chin held the knife at waist level and started walking toward the fractious group in the stern. He hated the blacks the ship carried crossing after crossing. It wasn't really them he hated, but rather himself, the captain and the rest of the crew. It was wrong to do what they did and he was ashamed of his part in it. He had been swallowing the evil he and his shipmates perpetrated on the innocent blacks and the regular meals of sin were eating holes in his soul. The blacks' chanting and singing was a perfect symbol of their innocence; it was a knife they turned in Chin's gut. The more beautiful they sang the more Chin's guilt grew.

"Shut up!" He screamed again, approaching the largest and best looking of the men in the stern, who was obviously a leader of some sort.

The strong black sang on, even when several others chained at his side became silent. He knew the yellow man wanted him to stop singing, but to stop singing would be to surrender his will to be a man.

The Archangel looked away from the scene as she repeated the terms of the challenge. "The total number of lives lost and saved will be counted after ten generations? And if more are saved than lost at man's own hand, mankind will continue as it has for an additional ten thousand years?"

"Exactly. But I think we should add a twist just to make it more interesting."

"What kind of twist?"

"We won't use all of mankind, only certain ones." The left corner of his mouth raised a sneer.

"Certain ones?" She knew there must be a catch. He had never been able to accept a contest that wasn't at least a little to his advantage.

"Just the ones wearing the ring . . . the ring on the man's hand that is holding the knife." He smiled and pointed to the ring on the middle finger of Chin's right hand.

The ring was a golden serpent that wrapped itself around the Chinaman's finger and bit its own tail. It was a fine piece of jewelry, hammered out by a shriveled old man with a keen eye and lifetime of patience. The snake had a glowing red eye that seemed to survey everything around it.

"You mean only *that* man or his children would determine the fate of mankind? I shall never agree to a test unless it includes all kinds of men and women."

"Not just him and his then." He sighed and his shoulders dropped a little. "Whoever comes into possession of the ring will have an equal opportunity to determine the fate of mankind."

The lovely angel turned involuntarily at the screams of the women and saw Chin plunge the knife to the hilt into the black man's stomach. The man did not scream as Chin pulled the knife down, cutting across the vital organs lying beneath the strong abdominal muscles. When she turned back, she saw the disappointment on the dark emissary's face. He was eager for a more slow and painful death, a death full of fear and submission, not strength and resistance.

"We shall have no say whatsoever in who wears the ring?" She wanted no rules unclear that he could later turn to his advantage.

"None," he answered, without taking his eyes off the carnage.

"Ten generations is not a very precise measure of time," she countered, not letting
herself look away from his repulsive presence. "The ring won't always be passed from fathers or mothers to their offspring, so how much time should be considered a generation?"

"All right, all right!" He was impatient, but refused to let his attention be diverted from the chaos. "We'll make it two hundred years—that's about ten generations, assuming that mankind will reproduce itself about every twenty years."

"Two hundred years from when? From now, eighteen-fifteen?" She was wary of a trick.

"Yes, from right now!" He didn't hesitate and didn't return her gaze. Then he smiled as the blacks screamed and pulled at their chains, trying to get free so they could help their wounded comrade.

"Then it's settled." She turned to see what was holding his attention.

Chin had gutted the slave in a fit of guilty rage and was overwhelmed by the heinous scene he had created.

"Beautiful, beautiful," the gleeful emissary said, putting his hand to his mouth and biting his knuckles as he watched in rapture. The young black man was praying to his god for strength as Chin stood on the entrails laying on the deck by his side.

She did not turn away from the sickening scene. "I love you, Rubba," she said, projecting herself across the ship. "Your loving faith in the Father shall not go unrewarded."

The disemboweled man felt her embrace, although no one else could see her. He smiled at the sound of her words and spoke to a cloudless blue sky that only he saw, "I love you now and forev...." The remaining life drained from him.

"You ruined it!" The dark angel was livid. "You ruined it!"

"It's your first victory. A life has been taken by the wearer of the ring, no matter how little you appreciate it, but mankind's goodness will prevail."

"Never!"

"Always," she countered. In that instant she departed the bowels of the ship in an almost imperceptible wink of blue light.

Over the following decades the ring would find its way to uncountable life and death struggles. It would bear witness to numerous killings that man would call justifiable, but would record only lives taken.

It is myopic—seeing only the actions of the wearer—and it remains unaffected by emotion, like the lens of a camera. It records neither the pain in a human heart that drives one to take a life, nor the love in a heart that leads one to sacrifice his own life to preserve that of another.

The ring is the ultimate impartial record keeper, sampling humankind randomly, through the actions of whoever possesses the ring, creating two kinds of representative links in the recorded historic chain of humankind's most important actions. One link would be buoyant like that of wood—of life giving—and the other like heavy wrought iron—of life taking. One link buoying the chain to float on an everlasting triad of earth, heaven and hell and the other weighing it to sink to a final apocalyptic accounting.

In the end, there will be a chain of two kinds of links, with no one link being any less important to the final density of the chain. Ultimately, the chain will either sink or float on the sea of God's law, the disposition of mankind resting on the final composition of the chain—a chain of individual links of humankind's actions. Actions recorded by the impartial red eye of the judgment ring.

THE CHINOOK RIVER PRINCESS

Chapter 1

Mary, age twelve, sat quietly on the weather-worn planks at the end of the dock. She stared intently at the cork bobber resting motionlessly on the mirror-like surface of the water. She held a coiled fishing line in her left hand. The air was perfectly still—the only break in the silence was the shrill call of a lone gull. The gull glided silently over the tall, multi-masted ships, exploring everything below with quick glances, its head moving in rapid jerks. The ships at anchor rode high in the water, in want of cargo. The bulk of their crews were ashore in the bawdy houses along the waterfront, conventional sailors trying to make up for the lonely months of isolation at sea.

Mary was oblivious to the shard of yellow-orange light piercing the distant horizon where the difference between heaven and earth had been imperceptible only a second before. The progressing sunrise washed the buildings on the wharf with a golden glow, but Mary didn't notice. Old Sam said the rockfish would be biting this morning and she was determined to catch one.

She turned with a start upon hearing a loud rumble behind her. Mr. Weed was setting the large oak trash barrel in front of his store. The lettering on the sign on the side of the two-story, weathered cedar building said BALTIMORE HARBOR GENERAL MERCHANDISE.

Mr. Weed was preparing for the brisk business he was sure to do later in the day—after the tobacco crops were sold. The tobacco-laden wagons would start rolling into the city before noon. Farmers would stack tons of freshly cured "bacca," as Mary's father called it, on the oak floor of the red tile-roofed open-air warehouse.

Mary's attention turned back to the water. Her heart started to pound as the bobber moved slowly away from the dock. Below the water's surface, a large striped bass pushed the crab-covered hook with its nose. Mary fought the urge to jerk the line, remembering what Old Sam told her: "Let'um have it; he'll play wid'it a li'l'. He'll gum it like a toofless old man, but if youse wait quiet-like, he'll take it and swims under de dock."

Old Sam knew his fish. At first the bobber just jerked a little and then stopped dead in the water. In a few seconds, it started moving slowly toward the dock before it disappeared abruptly below the surface. Mary waited what seemed an eternity before she yanked the line and when she finally did, it yanked back. The coil around her hand tightened, cutting off the circulation to her fingers. She had to lean back to keep from toppling head-long into the bay.

The rockfish swam close to the surface then dove deep, trying to get free from the enemy ripping at its mouth. Mary was thrilled when she saw the size of her opponent; it would bring a good price. She could do nothing but hold the line as the fish fought itself to exhaustion.

When the fish was finally spent, Mary stood and pulled the line up, hand-over-hand. Her prize swam in the air, trying to get away. She slung the fish onto the plank deck as soon as it cleared the edge. It flopped five or six times before settling down. The tail became still as it pumped its gill plates and gulped air.

She was elated but at the same time overwhelmed by the thought that the muscular beauty must die. She lifted the nine pounder by the fishing line, resting her elbows into her belly for support, and started walking toward Mr. Weed's store. It was heavy work; she had to stop every thirty feet for a brief rest. At sixty-five pounds, she was not much more than a match for the fish she was carrying.

When she reached the front of Weed's store she let the fish lay on the hard-packed clay roadway as she looked up and down the street. She waited about ten minutes, then her heart jumped when she spotted Albert Brooks, the old fish monger, at the end of the block. He wore a full, dark-green oilcloth apron over his light-blue cotton shirt and dark-blue trousers.

Mr. Brooks turned his cart onto Market Street and pushed it slowly toward Mary. His legs were bent like the wye of a slingshot and he walked with a side-to-side motion. In a pleasant musical chant he called out, "I have fresh fish this morn'. . . rock, croaker, eels, and crabs. Fresh fish today!"

She hoisted her prize again and struggled up the street. She looked quite ridiculous toting such a large fish while wearing high button shoes and a full-skirted dress.

Mr. Albert, as Mary called Albert Brooks, started grinning as soon as he saw her. "That's a beauty!"

"I caught it myself," she yelled, "off the pier!"

"Well, that's as pretty a rock as I've ever seen.," He took a few steps to meet her. "Let me take it." He reached out and lifted the burden from her exhausted arms.

"How much is it worth?" She was out of breath with excitement.

"I'd say it's worth two cents."

"Wow!" Then she said in almost a whisper, "That'll give me enough, I think."

"What'd you say?" the bandy-legged old man asked.

"Oh nothing."

"What are you going to do with the money?" He looked down the fish's mouth to see if he could retrieve the ingested hook.

"With the two cents you give me, I'll have fifty-one cents and I'm going to buy Papa a new pipe for his birthday."

"He home now?"

"No. . . not yet, but he'll be home any day now. He told me he'd get back the first of June."

"Great!" He was genuinely pleased for her. He reached behind his apron, into the pocket of his pants and retrieved a freshly-struck copper two-cent piece. It was an impressive coin, adorned by Miss Liberty staring out from a one-inch circle of stars. "Here you are, Miss Mary, and I'm sure your Papa will love his new pipe."

"Oh, thank you, Mr. Albert!" Her smile almost reached her ear lobes. She turned and ran home to fetch the rest of her savings, not bothering to retrieve her fishing line.

Home was a handsome white clapboard house with just a little gingerbread along the porch roof. There was a widow's walk just outside the master bedroom on the second floor. The house sat in a small yard but it wasn't crowded by other houses like was so often the case near

THE CHINOOK RIVER PRINCESS

the docks. It was high on the hill and had a clear view of the bay.

Mary ran up the front steps, taking them two at a time. She hit the front door so hard it was a wonder the glass panes didn't break. She ran through the hall and into the kitchen shouting, "Mrs. O! Mrs. O!"

"Mrs. Olsen was a sweet, slightly rotund, spirited forty-two-year-old lady with clear, wrinkle-free skin. Her brown hair was pulled back into a bun on the crown of her head. She had been cleaning the kitchen stove and doing laundry and several wisps of hair had come loose from the bun.

"What is it? What is it, Mary?" She feared that something terrible had befallen her little charge.

"Mrs. O, I caught the biggest fish you ever saw, just like Old Sam said, and I got a double penny for it from Mr. Albert!"

"Oh, thank the Lord," Mrs. O sighed. Then she sat heavily in one of the ladder-back chairs at the kitchen table. "You liked to scared me to death."

"Look." Mary held out her open palm and exhibited her newly acquired wealth.

"My, my. It's a real beauty, but why are you so excited? Your father left your allowance with me—ten cents a month. You've spent hardly any of it."

"Oh, Mrs. O, that's money that he earned and gave me—this is money that I earned to buy his birthday present!"

"Oh." Mrs. O was continually surprised by Mary's fully developed set of values and sensitivities. She never knew a child of Mary's age to be so mature and independent. She concluded shortly after she took the job of housekeeper for Mr. Harper and his little girl, that Mrs. Harper must have been quite a woman, very strong and loving, to have raised such a fine daughter. She learned from the neighbors that Mrs. Harper had slowly wasted away from consumption. She learned, too, that Mr. Harper had stayed home from the sea to nurse his wife himself for her last six months.

"I've got to show Old Sam!" Mary quickly turned and headed down the hall toward the front door. "He'll never believe I caught such a beauty. I'll have Mr. Albert show it to him to prove it."

She ran all the way to the wharf, where she had to wait for several tobacco-laden wagons to pass before she could cross the street to the tobacco auction warehouse. The warehouse was nothing more than a roofed area without walls that covered an entire city block. It wasn't at all fancy, but it served its purpose well—protecting the tobacco leaves from the weather without depriving them of the fresh air they needed to stay fresh.

As Mary ran toward the warehouse, she shouted, "Where's Old Sam?" to a wizened old black who was taking bundles of tobacco leaves from the back of a wagon and stacking them on a hand cart.

"Him's out back." He pointed through the dark interior of the warehouse toward the bay.

"Thanks!" She didn't break stride as she changed her direction to match that of the old black's pointing arm.

Old Sam was a very big black man, born and raised a slave in South Carolina. He was one of only a few blacks who had won their freedom; it was rare that an owner released a specimen as fine as Sam. As a young adult, Sam had been a breeding buck, one of the offspring of another prime buck owned by the Grande family of the Winelong plantation near Baton Rouge, Louisiana. Sam never saw his father but when he was a young man, Mr. Grande showed Sam his name in the breeding log he kept on reproducing slaves.

Although he couldn't read, Sam saw his father's name in the leather-bound book. It was recorded as Winelong's Buck Jim III, which meant that he was the third cash breeder named Jim on the Winelong plantation. Mr. Grande often said that Jim III was the most beautiful specimen he had ever laid eyes on. He described Jim to prospective breeding customers on other plantations as being as solid as a hundred-year oak, and standing almost as tall.

There were twenty-three women's names listed below Sam's father in the log and there was another name next to each of those. Since Sam couldn't read, Mr. Grande pointed out Sam's mother's name, Kinah, and his name, "Grande's buck Sam," next to hers. When Sam asked about the other words listed below his father's, Mr. Grande explained that Jim had been bred to twenty-two other women at Winelong plantation besides his mother and had fathered twenty-seven other children. Mr. Grande said the other children were fine healthy blacks, but Sam was almost a spitting image of his father.

When Sam came of age, Mr. Grande shipped him all around the south, earning a sizeable sum in stud fees for the plantation.

Although Mary was too young to hear the baser facts about slave life, Old Sam told her the story many times of how he came to be freed and she never tired of the tale. As he spoke, she saw the story unfold before her. She loved the deep bass tone of Sam's whispering voice.

Chapter 2

The way Sam told it, Mr. Grande had been having an affair with Mrs. Connant from a neighboring plantation for about three years. Mr. Connant was fifteen years older than Mr. Grande, who was no young man, being almost twenty years older than Mrs. Connant. The first Monday of every month, when Mr. Connant went to Savannah to replenish the plantation's supplies, Mr. Grande would slip over to pay Emily his respects.

Mr. Connant was old but not foolish; he had seen the way all the other plantation owners and their sons watched his Emily. Whenever he was away, he posted lookouts and spies at strategic points along the roads and in the forest on the northern side of the plantation. He figured that no one would risk passage through Terminal Swamp, which formed a five-mile-wide barrier to his land on the south.

But he underestimated the power of his Emily's attraction. He also underestimated the skills that men like Sam develop growing up beside the swamp. Mr. Grande had always been afraid of and hated the swamp, but neither his fear nor his hatred was as strong as his appreciation for Mrs. Connant's soft skin and coquettish smile.

On his last clandestine foray to the north, Mr. Grande sat in the bow as Sam, kneeling in the stern, poled the slim dugout through the restricted passages. The dugout moved slowly through narrow corridors flanked by massive cyprus festooned with Spanish moss, passing over uncountable large lily-covered pools of black water.

At one pool an alligator, as big as any that had ever grown in the swamps, slid from the river bank and into the tea-colored water when it heard the bottom of the dugout scrape across a submerged log. With an easy swish of its tail it moved swiftly and silently below the surface of the water.

The gator stopped and settled to the bottom of the pool. It waited until the boat was broadside to him and about fifty feet away, then beat its tail against the soft pool bottom and drove up toward the boat.

The gator's head pushed up fifty gallons of water as it rose to the surface, its body undulating powerfully as it snaked its way through the water, gathering speed. Sam and Mr. Grande heard and saw the 'gater at the same time. They stared in wide-eyed wonder, knowing there was nothing that could stop the charge. The gator continued its collision course with the boat, opening its mouth when it got within ten feet. A few seconds later, its immense jaws slammed closed, ripping a sizeable chunk from the right side of the boat. Sam held firmly to the gunnel but Mr. Grande was thrown head first into the water.

The 'gator submerged to the bottom of the pool for a few seconds and then rocketed to the surface. Its jaws slammed shut over Mr. Grande's torso, then dragged the portly slaver under the surface. The 'gator rolled with him, over and over, working to drown him so it could stuff him under a log to ripen for a future banquet. Sam sat dumbfounded before noticing Mr. Grande's skinning knife lying in the bottom of the boat. He grabbed the knife, which was a sharp as a freshly stropped straight razor, and jumped into the pool. The 'gator had stirred the rotting sediments on the bottom, changing the tea-colored water to that of coffee. Sam couldn't see three inches in the dark water, but somehow managed to find the trashing monster. He couldn't tell anyone exactly how he did it, but he split the 'gator jaw-to-tail with the knife.

Mr. Grande was so grateful that he gave Sam his freedom that evening. Sam told Mary how he knew that, given time, the greedy Mr. Grande might come to regret freeing him, and how he headed north the next morning.

When he first told her the story, Mary thought Sam might have made it up just to entertain her. Weeks later, when she saw the scars on his upper arm where the gator had raked him with his tightly spaced teeth, she had known what he said was not a story at all.

Sam was rolling freshly packed barrels to the loading platform when Mary ran up to him. "Look, Sam. . . look!" She held out her two-cent piece for him to admire. "I caught a huge rockfish, just like you taught me, and Mr. Albert gave me this for it."

"That must'ta been su-um fish!" He accentuated the word "some" by pronouncing it in two syllables.

"Oh, it was, it was, Sam. You should'a seen it."

"I wished I did, I shore wished I did."

"You can still see him," Mary said, her eyes wide. "Mr. Albert will have it on his cart after he cleans it."

"Well'en," Sam had an ear-to-ear grin on his broad face, "I'll just have a look-see when he comes back heah with his cart, I wills."

"You'll be surprised." Before rushing off, she added, "I've got to go tell Mr. Hawshorn that I got the money for Pa's pipe."

Mary stood in front of the shop window admiring the display of pipes before she went in. They were all beautiful, each distinctive in its own way.

A small brass bell mounted at the top of the door jamb rang when she pushed open the door. The proprietor came promptly from his shop in back.

"Miss Harper, you've come to admire my pipes again?"

"Yes, Mr. Hawshorn, but this time I've come to buy one. I saved fifty-one cents to get a nice one for Papa for his birthday."

"That's wonderful; you can buy most any pipe in my shop for fifty-one cents."

"That's good, 'cause I want to get a really special one ... which should I get?"

"That's a hard thing to say, because a pipe is a very special thing to a man. It becomes a part of him, like his arm or hand. It's very difficult to choose a pipe for another. What kind of pipes does he smoke?"

"He has all kinds, but his favorites are the ones with the crook in them."

"Ah, the Bents." He nodded knowingly. "I have to agree with him, the Bents are a special favorite of mine also. They have a low center of gravity. They don't put a strain on the jaw like the straights do, and they smoke dry."

"I don't know anything about pipes, Mr. Hawshorn, so tell me which are the good ones."

"They are all good, my dear," he replied, raising one eyebrow. "I don't make anything but good pipes, but there are ones that are special. They're special because of the briar they're made of. The highest quality pipes have grain that runs up the bowl like fingers," he said, picking up a bent that he had finished the day before. "See how the grain runs straight up the sides of the bowl?" He pointed to the dark lines in the wood. "This is such a nice grain it's called flame-grain. See how the grain run up the bowl like the flames of a fire?"

"Yes, I see." Mary was truly impressed, for she had never seen such a beautiful pipe. "Oh, this pipe is so beautiful." She held the product of Mr. Hawshorn's finest labor. "I want this one for Papa."

Mr. Hawshorn swallowed hard. It was made from the most perfect piece of briar that his hands had ever worked. He wanted it to be appreciated, but hadn't realized how he'd feel when someone proposed to remove it from his shop. The pipe was worth at least a dollar and to someone who could really appreciate it, maybe twenty-five cents more.

"It is a fine choice." He smiled his pain away. "Your Papa always appreciated my pipes. He'll really love this one." He reached under the counter to retrieve the small black walnut box that he had made for the special flame-grained Bent. He had lined the box with a piece of red Chinese silk that one of the captains had given him in exchange for one of his cheaper pipes.

"I'm afraid I couldn't afford the box too, Mr. Hawshorn, but it is awfully pretty."

"It comes with the pipe. You don't think I'd let a pipe like this just lay around anywhere, do you?"

"Oh, Papa will be so pleased with it!" She clasped her hands together at her mouth as she stared at the beautiful dark smooth box. "I can hardly wait to give it to him."

Even though Mr. Hawshorn held only half of what the pipe was worth, he was pleased, for money was only a part of the reward he sought for his labor. Mary's smiling face as she left his shop clutching the pipe as if it were the most prized object in her world made it all worth while.

By late that afternoon Mary had showed almost everyone in town the beautiful pipe she was going to give her father when he returned home. She had been especially eager to show Father O'Brien because he was an avid pipe smoker. He had been the parish priest for many years before Mary was born and had baptized her before her first birthday.

"It's a beauty." Father O'Brien held the Bent as he would hold a baby he was about to Christen, "This pipe is full of love—love of creation—and in the giving. Your father is going to cherish this piece of wood above all others—of that, you can be sure; not because it's such a magnificent piece of work, but because you gave it to him out of the love in your heart."

The Father placed the pipe back in its box and then with his hand resting on her shoulder, walked her down the aisle and through the large double door to the front steps, where he bid her God speed.

It was only three days after she bought the pipe that Mary saw her father's ship approaching the harbor. At first only the tops of the masts were visible, but when it grew close enough to see the deck, Mary knew it was the *Gloucester*. She ran home, retrieved the walnut box with its precious contents and returned to the dock before the deck hands had tossed the hawsers ashore.

She stood on the edge of the pier, loving the sounds of the ships at anchor. The water gurgled against the pilings and lapped against the sides of the wooden ships. The sounds all around her were the warm sounds that accompanied each of her father's returns. They were the prologue of the wonderful days that followed each of his returns—the happiest of days before he had to leave again.

Chapter 3

It seemed an eternity before the gangplank was set and the crew began to disembark.

Why does he always have to be almost the last one off? She thought. Doesn't he know how long I've been waiting?

When most of the crew had left the ship and she could wait no longer, she started across the gangplank and was stopped by a tall man that could have stood a bath and a shave.

"Where do you think you're going, Miss?"

"I'm going to fetch my Pa, sir, if that's all right."

"And who might you be?" He stood squarely in her path, his fists resting on his hips.

"I'm Mary Harper. My father is the first officer of this ship." Her pride showed clearly.

The tall dirty crewman's face suddenly became less menacing and his voice grew soft and warm. "Welcome aboard, Miss Harper." He offered his hand to steady her on the wobbly plank. "The officer's quarters are below and to the right." He indicated the stairway through the hatch.

"I know, thank you, Mr. . . . "

"Mr. Watson, Miss Harper," he said quickly, still holding her hand, "and it is my pleasure to meet the daughter of such a fine man and officer as your father."

THE CHINOOK RIVER PRINCESS

He looked at the small hand he held in his, rather than looking her in the eye.

"Thank you, Mr. Watson." Mary was sure he had not said something that he wanted to say and his eyes were red and watery, like a man who had too much to drink. Mary had seen plenty of red-eyed sailors from the ships who had too much to drink.

Mary went below, clutching the smooth dark box to her chest and turned to the right at the bottom of the ladder, just as Mr. Watson had told her. The passage was narrow and dark, except for the light that escaped from the open doorway of her Papa's cabin. It smelled like a dank hole that didn't get any light and the musty odor assailed her lungs, making it difficult to breathe.

She called out, fearing what might be lurking in the darkness before the doorway. "Papa, are you down here?" Hearing no response, she called out in a voice loud enough to scare any goblin hiding in the dark. "Father, it's Mary. Are you down here?"

From the doorway came a faint reply, "Come in, Mary, I need to talk to you."

She didn't recognize the voice, but it had been so long since she heard her Papa's voice that she thought it must be his. As she pushed the partially ajar door open, she could see a large man sitting at a small table in a very small room. He wasn't her Papa. The room was obviously her Papa's, for his pipes were resting in the combination humidor-pipe rack that her mother had given him the Christmas before she died. The sextant, bearing his engraved initials, was hanging from a special hook on the wall over the hammock.

The large man at the table was Captain Weiss. Mary had met him many times but she had never seen him so tired or dirty before. He looked as if he hadn't shaved for weeks and as though he didn't have the energy to lift the bottle of whisky sitting on the table in front of him.

"Captain Weiss, is my Papa here?"

The big man turned his head up and looked at the ceiling. Tears welled up in his swollen eyes.

Mary's heart began to race, pounding against the inside of her ribs. Something had happened to her father. She walked closer to the Captain. She wanted to know immediately, and yet wanted to stand there forever waiting for the answer rather than to hear it. So long as he didn't speak, there was a chance that her Papa was fine.

The Captain drew her to him with his massive arms and started blubbering on her little shoulder. In response, she began to sob also, her sobbing quickly changing to a high-pitched wail. The Captain didn't have to tell her that her father was no longer among the living. When her mother died, she had to be told many times before she understood. Having seen the suffering of adults at the death of a loved one, she only too well grasped even the unspoken words.

After a time, the Captain picked her up and placed her in her father's hammock, where she continued to wail between spells of whimpering.

The Captain finished what remained in the whisky bottle without bothering to complicate his efforts with a glass. Then he talked about his first officer, the late Mr. Harper. It seemed that he was talking to the world in general, or to himself, rather than to Mary. "Your father," he began, "was the finest first officer I ever had. He was always respectful and served me with absolute loyalty, even when he disagreed with me."

Mary couldn't understand what the captain was saying most of the time, but understood that he felt the loss of her father almost as deeply as she. As she lay in the hammock, her thoughts turned to her mother and how her Papa had loved her.

She didn't have a chance to really get close to him because he was away from home so much. She wanted to be close to him but just about the time they would get comfortable together, after he had been home for a week or two, he would have to ship out again. He was a wonderful man, but she hardly knew him. He was away so long that she would forget what he looked like and when the crew came off of the ship, it would be several moments before she recognized him. She knew when she came today that she would have trouble recognizing him and now the faded memory of his face would continue to dim in his perpetual absence. When her attention returned to the present, the captain was still spilling his emotions.

". . . then a tremendous wave struck the old girl broadside and snapped the upper stay on the main mast. Your father yelled to the men to get out of the way of the falling rigging, but they were too tired to hear. Your father, in no more than four strides, reached the men and pushed them clear." The captain stopped and placed his right hand over his eyes as if to block his view of the scene, but the picture was inside his head and couldn't be blocked by the expedient raising of hand to eyes. "The stay struck him on the back of the neck and he was gone in the very instant it happened. He was gone without a sound, without a word, and without my telling him how much he meant to me."

The big man sat staring at the bottle on the table with tear-blurred vision and Mary thought about what he said, about not having the chance to tell him how much he meant to him. Her father would never see the beautiful pipe she had bought for his birthday. Did anyone on the ship wish him a happy birthday, or even know he had a birthday two months ago? She stared woefully at the walnut box sitting on the table.

Her mother had been the closest person in her life and when she died, Mary consoled herself with the periodic presence of her father. Now he was gone and she had no family. The depth of her despair was too great and she drifted off to sleep with the musty smell of the cabin in her nostrils. The Captain carried her home as she slept. He was not too steady on his feet but she was sleeping too soundly to notice. He put her on her bed. Mary didn't even stir when Mrs. O undressed her and covered her with a sheet.

Mary slept fitfully. She dreamed, again and again, that she was aboard the *Gloucester* looking for her father. She was surprised when she finally awoke in her own bed at home.

It was just a dream, she thought, as she bolted to an upright position. As soon as she sat up, she saw the dark box on the night table. Next to it was her father's humidor. There was also his little pine jewelry box in which he kept his few prized adornments. She retrieved the small rectangular pine box from where she lay, lifted the lid and peered inside. She started crying noiselessly. Tears squeezed out of her tightly closed eyes and her

THE CHINOOK RIVER PRINCESS

mouth twisted in anguish, giving her face the appearance of a tragic Greek mask.

After a few minutes she calmed and reached into the box. She took out her father's wedding ring, which she slipped over her too-small finger. Next she took out her father's gold pocket watch, which he received from her grandfather. She set the watch upon her gown-covered chest and took out the other gold ring. It had always rested on the second finger of her father's right hand.

She remembered that when anyone commented on the ring, her father would tell them the story of how one afternoon when he was at the helm of the ship, he spotted a man hanging onto a piece of flotsam bobbing up and down in a calm sea. He told how he brought the ship about and dispatched several hands in a rowboat to pick the man up. The man was a Chinese named Chin. He told his rescuers how the slaves on his sunken ship had revolted, killed most of the crew and then, out of ignorance, sank the ship under themselves by knocking holes through the hull. He told how he hid in a galley cupboard and how he almost didn't make it to the ocean's surface as the ship sank below the waves. Her father told of how the man named Chin gave him the ring out of gratitude for saving his life.

She remembered that her father always proudly told the story. He said that he was sure there was some kind of divine providence that made him see that lone man on the surface of the ocean that day.

She couldn't tell that the ring was very old—it looked as if it had been just made. It was an unusual design—a snake made of one long tapered cylinder of gold, coiled to encircle the finger. The cylinder's ends met on the top of the ring. One end, the serpent's head, devoured the other, the serpent's tail. A very small ruby was set deeply into the serpent's head.

Mary slipped the ring over the second finger of her right hand, as her father had worn it. She was surprised that it fit. It seemed impossible, but it fit her little finger as perfectly as it fit her father's finger. Her father's finger was at least half-again as large as hers. She admired the way the ring looked on her finger, unaware of its importance to mankind.

Over the next several weeks, Mary could be seen strolling the higher streets of the city, away from the docks. She always appeared deep in thought, as if she were trying to discover some illusive truth.

Mary had few friends. When she lost her mother, the other kids didn't want to hear or think about her grief. They wanted to do fun things and she had put a damper on their fun. She had been forced to settle for adult companionship because only adults could handle her moods and accept her grief. With the loss of her father, Mary lost what little remained of her childhood. She became a hardened little woman.

Chapter 4

A little more than two months after the *Gloucester* sailed
into the harbor, Mr. Kirby, the president of the First Bank of Baltimore, came to visit Mary and Mrs. O. Mrs. O invited him into the sitting room for tea and biscuits.

"I have been appointed the executor of Mr. Harper's estate and have come to advise you of the disposition of that estate." He sat comfortably in her father's favorite chair and that made Mary uncomfortable..

"I understand." Mary put on her best adult voice, but didn't understand at all.

She was not, in any way, prepared to deal with the likes of Mr. Kirby. He had decided that a little girl had no business owning a lovely home and a sizable savings account at the bank. He was from the old school, which taught that such rewards were due only to those who had paid for them with years of sweat and pain, or to those who knew how to take such rewards from others.

"Good, Mary. I'll tell you how your father's estate rests at the moment. He had a savings account in the bank which presently holds one hundred and fifty dollars and twenty-three cents," the dapper read from a small ledger he held in his lap, "and the equity in this home. The home is worth about fifteen hundred dollars, but Mr. Harper borrowed twelve hundred dollars last year, using the house as collateral. That means that if the house can be sold for fifteen hundred dollars, Mr. Harper's estate will have a net value," looking up from his ledger, he smiled, "of approximately four hundred and fifty dollars."

"Four hundred and fifty dollars." Mary put her hands to her cheeks in surprise. "I'm rich, aren't I?" She turned to Mrs. O.

"Four hundred fifty dollars, and she loses the house?" Mrs. O's eyes were daggers.

"Yes. She'll be the most wealthy little girl in town." Mr. Kirby beamed..

"Lose the house," Mary repeated, truly perplexed. "what do you mean, lose the house?"

"Well," Mr. Kirby said in his most authoritative demeanor, "the house will have to be sold to pay off the loan for which the house was collateral."

"What's collateral?" Mary was overwhelmed by the terminology thrown at her.

"Collateral, is what one gives up in order to pay back what one borrows when one cannot make payments on it."

"I don't believe my father would borrow money . . . he didn't believe in it," Mary remembered conversations that he had with her mother.

"Well, he did borrow twelve hundred dollars last year and here is the loan paper." He testily produced a one-page document. It bore a signature that neither Mrs. O or Mary could be sure was Mr. Harper's, since they weren't accustomed to seeing his signature. "I'm putting the house up for auction in one week. You'll have one week after that to make other arrangements. If you don't have a place to store everything in the house." He spoke without emotion. "I suggest that you auction the contents at the same time the house is auctioned. It's the only way to dispose of so much in a short time and it's the best way to get a good price for everything."

"If I'm rich, why must we sell the house?" Mary was ringing her hands in despair.

"You don't have enough money to pay off the amount of money your father borrowed." Mr. Kirby made little effort to console her.

"If I give you all of the money, can I keep the house?"

"If you paid back only part of the money, Mary," he said quietly, "you'd have to make interest payments on the money you didn't pay back, and you have no income to make payments."

"That's it!" Mrs. O shouted into Mr. Kirby's face. "Mr. Harper couldn't have borrowed any money from the bank because he was away for up to seven or eight months at a time and he didn't have me make any payments to the bank so there was no loan, Mr. Kirby."

Mr. Kirby turned a bright red but held his tongue for a few moments until his temper cooled. "Mr. Harper made special arrangements with me to pay his back payments whenever he came into port."

"I'll just bet he did, I just bet he did." Mrs. O's voice was dripping with sarcasm. Mr. Kirby stood. "Good day, ladies. I know this is hard, but it's the way of business." Then he walked to the front door and left.

Mrs. O was livid and could only pace up and down the hall muttering to herself while Mary sat quietly in the parlor, too stunned to move.

"What am I going to do Mrs. O?" Mary asked absently. "I have nowhere to go."

"Don't worry your little head about it." She moved to Mary and took her head to her bosom. "You'll stay with me and Mr. O and ours before I'll let you be put in the town home."

Mary's blood ran cold at the words "town home." She had heard enough stories from several children who lived at the home. They had only grizzly tales of their life in that white clapboard prison.

The following weeks were like a bad dream. Before she had adjusted to being an orphan, she found herself homeless. Three weeks after her father's ship came back to port without him she stood in the small front yard of what used to be her home, among a crowd of bargain hunters. She had never seen an auction before and through the remainder of her years, would never be able to stomach one again. A small balding man stood on a foot stool, calling for bids on the little that remained of the links to her past.

It was mid-August and the hot air blew across the open water of the bay, picking up enough moisture to make life in the harbor area a living hell. Mary was soaking wet in her long dress. Her damp hair clung to the back of her neck.

"Next we have a chestnut dinner table and six chairs. What am I bid? Do I hear a dollar?" The auctioneer called out in a sing-song banter. "Who'll start the bidding at a dollar? Ninety-five cents, ninety cents . . . we have ninety. The bid starts at ninety cents. Do I hear ninety-five? Ninety-five!" He pointed to someone near the corner of the porch. "Now a dollar, do I hear a dollar? Do I hear a nickel more? Do I hear one-oh-five. . . now one-ten? Do I hear one-ten? Come now, gentlemen," he said in mock disbelief. "This is the best table and chair grouping I've seen offered in a long time and you can't let

THE CHINOOK RIVER PRINCESS

it go for that price, even if you don't need it. Even if you have to give it to your mother-in-law . . ." he said with a chuckle. "You can't let it get away for that price. Come on, one-ten . . . one-ten . . .. Well, folks, in that case, it is sold to Mr. Hanks for one-oh-five. You, Mr. Hanks, just got one fine deal."

Mary was on the verge of collapse; she was dizzy from the heat and the blinding sunlight. Watching the table being sold like just any old thing wrenched her heart. Some of her fondest memories were of the dinners at that table just after her father had returned from the sea. He would spend his first day home at that table, eating her mother's cooking and telling of his months on the ocean. During those times, Mary felt warm and part of something very special.

Whenever her mother came too close, her father would reach out and, grabbing her by whatever he could get hold of, pull her mother to him, smothering her with kisses and hugs. Mary learned that she, too, could get some of the loving if she moved within his reach. She was reluctant to do so at first because after months at sea he was a stranger. It was always several hours before she would accept the fact that the jovial man was her father and slowly advance to share in his warmth.

The auctioneer moved from the table to her mother's dresser. Mary could stand no more. She turned and fought her way through the throng to the street and then ran from the nightmarish scene. She ran as if the devil himself were on her heels and by the time she reached the bottom of the hill, she was gasping for air. Mercifully the sing-song calls of the auctioneer had faded to almost inaudible.

Chapter 5

After losing the only home she'd ever known, Mary moved into the Olsen house where she was almost accepted by the Olsen's six children. She got along with the youngest two girls but Betty, the oldest, didn't appreciate having another female in the house. The boys definitely didn't appreciate having another girl in their midst—that is, the two youngest boys didn't. Clem, the oldest, liked the idea of Mary's coming from the start. He had met Mary and knew she was much more mature and sensible than his sisters.

Clem was thirteen when Mary moved in. He was tall and thin, with dark hair, blue eyes, and a quiet manner. At school he always had a friendly word for her.

Her first Saturday at the Olsen house was bitterly sweet. Seeing Mr. and Mrs. O together was painful because it brought back the memories of her own parents together.

That Saturday, Mrs. O walked Mary to her new home. Mary felt an overwhelming dread as she climbed up the front steps of the Olsen house beside Mrs. O. Each stair she climbed brought her closer to a totally different life from what she had known. Her own home had given her a tremendous feeling of security—all the wonderful memories kept her warm and safe. She climbed the Olsen's stairs that morning to a new and alien life, a future of unknowns.

THE CHINOOK RIVER PRINCESS

She matched Mrs. O's steps stride for stride, climbing the gray-painted steps of the Olsen house. A large glass window covered most of the top half of the front door and just below the glass was a doorbell lever, with the bell mounted on the inside. Pushing down on the spring-returned lever would spin an eccentric clapper against the bell, causing it to ring in a tone of middle C. Mary noticed at once that the door needed painting; the white paint was chalky and cracked. Even though her father spent most of his time at sea, the Harper house had never been in need of fresh paint.

Mary stood back a few feet as Mrs. O turned the front doorknob. She pushed the door open and stood aside, waiting for Mary to enter first. As Mary stepped across the threshold she was immediately aware of the house's odor. Every house, that is every inhabited house, has its own distinctive odor. It's the combination of all the odors of all the individuals who live there and all of the things they do. The odor in the Owens' house was sightly sweet and warm. It smelled of all the meals that Mrs. O had cooked over the years, an aromatic blend of thyme, rosemary, cardamom, savory, ginger, cinnamon, nutmeg and cloves. There was also the smell of lye soap. Mrs. O always did her washing on the large back porch off the kitchen.

Mary became a changed person after her ordeal. She had become more introverted and now found most conversation trivial. Everything seemed to lean toward insignificant in light of the magnitude of events that had befallen her. What could possibly seem important next to losing her mother, then her father, and finally her home and everything in it?

In addition to being emotionally overwhelmed, she was physically exhausted. The emotional turmoil sapped her physical strength and left her drawn and haggard. She was like the flame of an oil lamp low on fuel—she no longer gave off a brilliant light. Mrs. O didn't help Mary shed her gloomy outlook with her constant comments on how she thought Mr. Kirby had stolen what was rightfully Mary's. Mary learned to loath the sight of Mr. Kirby and the bank.

In the four years that followed her father's death, Mary came to look upon Sam as a surrogate father. She spent hours in the evenings sitting with the aging black sage on the front porch of his ramshackle cottage south of the town.

Whenever Mary had a particularly bad day, Sam was there to put things into proper perspective. When she would cry about the way some of the other girls treated her, which was not any different than they treated each other from time to time, Sam lent a sympathetic ear. Then he'd relate some really bad experience that had befallen him or one of his friends down on the plantation. Everything is judged by comparing it to everything else, and Sam's stories always made her realize that her problems were rather insignificant when compared to what others experienced.

Mary had lost both of her parents, but both losses were unavoidable. She realized that such a loss was more tolerable than having one's family broken up and sold at the whim of a slave owner. Through Sam's eyes she saw the world in a different light than other girls her age. She understood the true meaning and importance of freedom and self-determination.

The years passed like horses in a parade; all seemed quite similar and unspectacular. Before Mary knew it, she was sixteen. Like most women of sixteen, she had no interest in sixteen-year-old boys. Mary was an attractive young woman with firm bumps and soft hollows in the proper places and amounts. She had developed a vacant, unconcerned look that excited men who passed her on the street.

Most of the young men in town were smitten with Mary and Trent Kirby, the banker's son, was especially so. He was a fine looking young man of twenty-three. Had he not been Banker Kirby's son, Mary would have enjoyed having him come courting.

Mary worked as a sales clerk in Mr. Weed's General Store. One day, she was folding work pants when Trent walked up and started examining the pants on the table.

"Good afternoon, Miss Harper." Trent tried to act nonchalant. He picked up a pair of pants and began inspecting the stitching.

"Afternoon, Mr. Kirby. Have you started wearing work pants over at the bank now?"

"No, but I do occasionally do some work outside that isn't best done in a suit."

"Ah, you do work, do you? I thought you'd be more like your father."

"And what does that mean?"

"I thought you'd just take whatever you want."

"My father worked hard for everything he has, Miss Harper."

"Not quite everything. He didn't have to work at all for the house you Kirby's live in."

"Just what does that mean?"

"It means he stole the house from me."

"The house rightfully belonged to the bank; your father didn't pay properly on his loan."

"My father never borrowed a dime from the bank!" Mary threw the pair of pants she was holding down on the table. "Your father forged the loan papers."

"My father is an honorable man and I resent your claims otherwise." Trent's grip was crushing the pants he held in his fists.

"Resent them all you like, Mr. Kirby. Your father's nothing but a common thief. No, not a common thief—a rich and powerful thief."

"He is not a thief but what has he got to do with me?"

"You are your father's son."

"I am my own man and if you would but just go out with me once, you'd see that."

"I'd see nothing of the sort and I'd sooner go out with an eel than the likes of you, Trent Kirby."

Mr. Weed heard Mary's raised voice and came out of the stock room, carrying several pairs of the work gloves he had been counting. "What's going on here, Mary? Why are you arguing with a customer?"

"Mr. Kirby's not a customer. He's just here to bother me."

"I am a customer. I was looking for a pair of work pants and I'm not used to being treated so."

THE CHINOOK RIVER PRINCESS

"Apologize, Mary, and help Mr. Kirby find a pair of pants that will suit his needs."

"I'll not apologize and I'll not help him with anything."

"You will apologize immediately or you will be fired."

"I will not apologize."

Mr. Weed stood perfectly still, hoping he would not have to let Mary go. She was his best clerk but other customers were staring at the trio. "You're fired!" Mr. Weed finally blurted.

Mary's face hardened and she turned on her heel and promptly bumped into Mrs. Conners, who was standing just a few feet away at the shirt table. Mary didn't say a word to Mrs. Conners. She stepped around her, walked quickly to the door, and then outside.

"You did the right thing." Trent nodded to Mr. Weed. "You have to be firm with help or they'll take advantage of you every time."

Mr. Weed glared daggers at Tent, then he turned and marched back to the storeroom. He threw the gloves down on the floor. "Damnation!" he shouted through clenched teeth.

Mary walked to the tobacco barn. She had to see Sam. She felt out of control of her life, as if she were starting to float away from everything she knew. Sam was the anchor to bring her back to earth and make things right again.

Sam was on the loading platform in the rear of the tobacco barn, hammering lids on tobacco casks with an eight-pound wooden mallet. Rivulets of sweat ran down the back of his neck and down his back, soaking his tan cotton pants. He stopped hammering when he saw Mary making her way down the narrow isle lined with casks. Sam slammed the butt of the hammer's handle down on the top edge of the cask, forcing the mallet head to seat more firmly on the handle shaft. He did it twice, stalling to give Mary time to reach him. Mary had sensitive hearing and he didn't want to hurt her ears.

"What's a matta, Miss Mary? You looks like you lost a bess fren'."

"Oh, Sam, Mr. Weed fired me because I got in an argument with Trent Kirby and I wouldn't apologize."

"He's dat banker's son, ain't he?"

"That's him."

"Miss Mary, you gonna hafta learn you cants go arguin' with the likes of a banker's son, no ma'am."

"I couldn't help it, Sam. The man just gets under my skin."

"What's ya gonna do now?"

"I have to look for another job."

"You'll fine one, Miss Mary. Youze a good worker."

Mary felt better after only a few encouraging words from Sam; she always did. She left the tobacco barn and headed up Main Street. A sign advertising for a sales clerk hung in the window of Armentrout's Haberdashery store, so Mary went right in.

Mary found Mrs. Armentrout on a ladder in the rear of the store, putting a large hat box on a shelf. Mrs. Armentrout was a pretty woman, about forty years old. Her hair was pulled back in a bun and split-frame reading glasses rested low on her nose. She wore a long, full dress. Mary stood silently until Mrs. Armentrout put the box on the shelf and looked down at her.

"Mrs. Armentrout, I'm Mary Harper. I'd like to be your new sales clerk."

"You work at Weed's Store don't you?"

"I did until today, Ma'am."

"You quit?"

"Yessem." She realized that Mrs. Armentrout would learn the truth soon enough and quickly changed her answer. "Although some might say I was fired."

"Fired?"

"Yessum."

"And what, pray tell, would make a fine man like Mr. Weed fire you?"

"Mr. Trent Kirby started an argument with me and I refused to apologize to him, so Mr. Weed said that if I didn't apologize to Mr. Kirby he would fire me."

"So you didn't apologize."

"No, Ma'am."

"Well, my dear. I sell many hats to the Kirby family and their friends, so I can't see how I could afford to hire you. You do understand, don't you?"

Mary looked down at her feet. "Yessem. Good-bye, Mrs. Armentrout."

"Goodbye, Mary. I would be happy to hire you, if I could."

"Yessem." Mary turned quickly and walked out of the store before Mrs. Armentrout could see her tears.

Chapter 6

As was usual that evening at supper, Sally, Susan, Betty, and Mary sat on one side of the long dining table, Billy, Jimmy, and Clem sat on the other side, with Mrs. and Mr. O at each end. The boys ate several large helpings of roast pork and potatoes, while the girls just picked at their food. Mr. O was unusually silent during the meal.

Mary pushed the food around her plate until Mrs. O asked, "You're not eating, Mary?"

"I'm not hungry tonight."

"What's wrong? Tell us."

"Well, if you must know, I was fired today."

"Fired? For what?"

"Trent Kirby started an argument with me and I refused to apologize when Mr. Weed told me to."

"That's right, Mary. Don't you ever cow toe to those Kirbys. They're all no damned good."

"That's no way to talk in front of the kids, Sarah." Mr. O had always been adamant about not swearing in front of the kids.

"When it comes to the Kirbys, John, there aren't any words too bad for the kids to hear."

Mr. O was silent through the rest of the meal. He pushed the food around his plate like the girls did. After supper he went out on the porch for a smoke. Mrs. O usually joined her husband on the porch but after their

THE CHINOOK RIVER PRINCESS

words she went to her room to read. Sally, Susan, and Betty played a card game in the parlor, while Billy and Jimmy talked with the neighbor boys in the back yard. Clem went courting to Lucy Luck's.

Mary walked out onto the porch after she finished washing the dishes. It was a glorious evening. There was a cool breeze and the setting sun bathed the whole harbor in a pink glow. Mr. O was rocking gently in the porch swing, looking out over the ships docked at the wharf below. Mary sat on the top step of the porch with her feet on the next lower step, her arms wrapped around her long dress, crinolines and legs. She put her chin on her knees and watched a three-masted schooner leave the harbor with the off-shore breeze.

"You know, Mary, I haven't told Mrs. O yet, but I lost my job three days ago."

"Why?"

"There's not so much need for ships carpenters now that they started using all these new copper chemicals to treat the wood—not nearly so much rotten wood to replace these days. I'm getting old so they let me go first."

"That's not fair . . . not fair at all."

"It doesn't seem fair to me either, Mary, but that's the way it is."

"What's going to happen?"

"I don't rightly know. I've been all over the city looking for work, but there are too many carpenters out of work right now."

"Can you do something else?"

"What else can I do? I've been a ship's carpenter for close to twenty years. I don't know anything else."

"I'll find another job and you can have everything I make."

"The two dollars you pay us every month is more than enough for your keep and you're really a daughter to us. You shouldn't be paying us anything."

"I want to, Mr. O, and if you don't find another job soon, you'll be needing everything I can earn—everything the others earn also."

"I can't live off my children."

"Pride is a sin, Mr. O. Remember what the Bible says."

"The Bible doesn't know what it is to be a man without a job."

"Don't say things like that, Mr. O. Things will work out, you'll see."

"I don't know how. I have to pay the bank twelve dollars each month and if I don't, the bank will take the house."

Mary's jaw dropped and she exhaled loudly. It was as if someone had kicked her square in the back with the toe of a boot.

"How much do you owe?"

"About thirteen hundred dollars."

All the feelings of her father's passing washed over her again. She felt that she had to raise her head and stretch her neck to keep above the sea of emotions that boiled around her. She stood up and went to her room. She lay awake until dawn, wondering what would become of the Olsens.

Mr. Hawshorn hired Mary to sell pipes in his shop as soon as he heard that Mr. Weed had fired her. He hired

THE CHINOOK RIVER PRINCESS

her as an old friend but was confident she would be an asset to his operation; she loved pipes and learned quickly. She ran the front of the store, showing cigars and pipes to customers, while Mr. Hawshorn worked undisturbed in his shop behind the store. It was amazing how much more he could accomplish by not having to stop work to attend to his customers. Mary sold more than Mr. Hawshorn had because she could spend the time needed to show his pipes to their best advantage. No man can sell wares as easily to another man as a beautiful woman.

Mary was showing Judge Warren a selection of Mr. Hawshorn's finest Bents. When she looked up upon hearing the door open. Her blood froze.

"Good afternoon, Mary." Trent Kirby shut the door behind him.

"Good afternoon, Mr. Kirby. I'll be with you in a few minutes." She turned her attention back to Judge Warren. "As I was saying, this one is my favorite. It's one of Mr. Hawshorn's finest briars; the amber stem will last for years. When it does finally wear out, Mr. Hawshorn will replace it with another at no cost."

"Well, Mary, it's a beauty and that's an offer I can't turn down."

"Fine, I'll wrap it for you. That will be one dollar and four bits, Judge."

"It would be a bargain at twice the price. Here's a two," he said, handing Mary a two-dollar gold piece, "and keep two bits for your trouble."

"I couldn't, Judge. It was no trouble at all. I love talking with you."

"I won't accept no for an answer. You take the twenty-five cents and I'm all the richer for your conversation. Do you know how pleasurable it is talking to a beautiful young lady like yourself?"

"No, Judge." Mary blushed as she handed the judge his quarter change.

"Well, take my word for it."

"Thank you, Judge, it's greatly appreciated."

The judge nodded to Trent as he pulled open the door and stepped out onto the wooden walkway. Trent nodded back. "Afternoon, Judge."

"Well, what can I do for you, Mr. Kirby?"

"You can show me some pipes like you showed the judge."

"You don't smoke a pipe. I'm sure you're not here to shop, so what is it you want?"

"I thought you should know that Mr. Olsen is falling behind in his loan payment for the house."

"I thought he was making the payments."

"Not fully. He tries, paying as much as he can scrape together every week, but he's about thirty dollars in arrears now."

"So what does that mean?"

"It means that shortly the bank will have to foreclose his loan."

"You mean steal his house?"

"No. It's just the way the banking business is. If one doesn't make the agreed payments, one forgoes one's property. It's very simple and straightforward."

"The Olsen's will be out on the street?"

"That's really up to you."

"Up to me?"

"It would be very difficult, if not impossible, for me to put a woman I'm courting out on the street."

Mary studied Trent's face. He was a fine looking man and there was nothing in his eyes that betrayed the sinister soul behind them.

"And just what would your courting consist of?"

"Your accompanying me on walks in the park and to dinners at the finest restaurants in Baltimore."

"Nothing more?"

"Nothing more. I'm sure you'll find me pleasurable company, if you give me just half a chance to talk to you. The hostilities you feel for my father will slowly disappear if you just get to know me."

"You promise you will not let the bank throw the Olsen's out in the street?"

"Yes, if you give me a fair opportunity to show you that I'm not the ogre you make me out to be."

"All right, Mr. Kirby,"

"You won't be sorry, Ma—" Mary cut him off. "If you try to take any liberties, Mr. Kirby, it's you who will be sorry."

"I'm a perfect gentleman, I assure you." Trent bowed low from the waist.

Sam was not pleased when Mary told him about her agreeing to see Trent Kirby. "Dats a bad idear, Miss Mary. That Trent Kirby is a man-about-town, he is, if youse knows what I means."

"If you mean he's courting a number of ladies in town, I know."

"I means he's a courtin' a mite more dan the ladies."

"What do you mean?"

"I means he ben spendin' time at dat dare baudy house down by de docks, that's what I means."

"You mean with ladies of the evening?"

"I don't means no ladies of no evenin'. I means dose anytime-you-got-cash-deys-a-ready women."

"I don't think so, Sam. The Kirby's can't afford to be seen frequenting a . . . a house of ill repute."

"I doesn't knows nuttin 'bout no ills reputes or what else, but I heerd he spends a heap a time in dat house down by de docks. An what's a bankerman froms a rich fambily doin a courtin' an orphan lady livin' with a housekeeper an her fambily anyhows? He ain't up to no good, Miss Mary. Minds my word, he's up ta no good and youse betta watch yoself."

"I'll be careful, Sam." She smiled and nodded. "Don't you worry."

The Olsen's weren't any more happy about Mary allowing Trent Kirby to court her than Sam was. That evening after supper, Mrs. O paced the kitchen floor while Mr. O sat at the table turning a silver dollar edge-over-edge, making an irritating metallic clicking sound.

"What's got into you, girl?" Mrs. O asked as Mary washed the supper dishes.

"Nothing's got in to me. What's wrong with allowing a banker to court me?"

"A Kirby?"

"He's not his father."

"He's cut from the same bolt of cloth." Mr. O spoke without looking up.

Mrs. O chimed in, "I wish you would think some more about this, Mary.".

"He's not like his father." Mary's voice grew louder as she tried to be convincing.. "He's not trying to throw us out of this house, is he?"

Mr. O was silent only a moment. "Is that it, Mary? Are you gonna court Trent so the bank doesn't throw us out of this house? Tell me it isn't so."

"No. I just was making the point that Trent's not like his father, that's all."

"I think I'm going to be ill." Mrs. O sat down at the table and sank in her chair like one of the sheets she tosses in the air while making a bed.

"I can't believe we've been reduced to this by losing my job," Mr. O shook his head.

Mary was quick to respond, not wanting Mr. O to feel responsible. "Just cut all this talk out. I'm going to let Trent Kirby court me and that's all there is to it. I don't know how long it will last. Things may get better in a little while, or maybe he'll decide I'm no fun to court."

Mrs. O's response was just as quick. "Now there's a happy thought."

Father O'Brien grew concerned for Mary's well-being from the very moment he learned of the loss of her father and his concern had steadily waxed over the ensuing years. Like the others, Father O'Brien became uneasy when he learned of Mary's plans to court Trent Kirby.

The good Father realized it was time that the little Mary he had baptized so many years before be given in marriage to someone worthy of her love. Someone strong enough to hold on to it; someone far away from Trent Kirby and Baltimore. It was, therefore, with much joy that he read a letter from Bret McGrath. It seemed that

Bret had a dear friend and neighbor, John March, who had lost his wife and like Bret, was anxious to acquire a religious, deserving woman, sight unseen.

Bret had grown up in Father O'Brien's parish and departed for the western frontier fifteen years before. He left as a lad of ten with his family and had become one of the first of many young men to adopt the western way of life. The McGrath family were very devout Catholics but the good Father had worried about their religious commitment in the absence of civilization. It appeared that he needn't have worried, for a letter he received from Bret five years before made it clear that the McGrath family had not let the primitive West subdue their religious spirit. The letter was Bret's plea for a good Catholic wife to fill the terrible void in his life. Father O'Brien thought of Beth Talbot, who had been one of his parishioners in Connecticut before he came to Baltimore. He wrote to her. She was more than willing to emigrate for the right man. 'Twas a match made in heaven.

From Bret's description of John March in his letter, Father O'Brien was sure he would be a perfect husband for Mary. It was the perfect opportunity for her; the good Father was sure that John March was just as good a man as Bret McGrath. Father O'Brien saw that the good Lord had finally given him the means to get Mary away from the men of the sea and the town that kept her memories festering like a septic wound.

Chapter 7

Life in the West could be harsh, but the father knew that the Lord had tempered Mary well for such hardship. He scorched her soul with the fire of suffering and then quenched it with the oil of despair.

Mary's reaction to Father O'Brien's proposal was immediate: "Never. I could never leave Baltimore. It's my home. Why would I go out West where there are savages, wild animals and smelly fur trappers?"

"There's a world that you can't even imagine out there. I've read that there are herds of over a million buffalo that quietly roam the plains and sunsets too beautiful to imagine." He was whispering as he stared at the picture he had created in his mind. "There are noble Indians who wear beautiful hats of feathers and the men are closer to the hand of God."

"It sounds as if you should go, Father, rather than I."

"My parish is here and I am too old to make such a journey. Besides, 'tis a wife John March needs, not a priest."

"I should travel thousands of miles," she asked, furrowing her brow, "to marry a man I've never laid eyes on?"

"In his letter Bret McGrath assured me that John March is a strong, good looking Catholic gentleman, clear of eye and mind. He said he would send two thousand dollars to cover the cost of the trip and any debts that his future wife may have taken upon herself. I'm sure you could do worse."

"I'm sure I shall, but at least it'll be my doing."

The good Father left the Olsen home with a profoundly sad heart, for he had not imagined that Mary wouldn't be as eager to go as he. He would have given the page-turning finger on his right hand to be her age and have the opportunity to confront God's unspoiled wilderness.

In the weeks that followed Trent did take Mary to the finest restaurants in Baltimore, and true to his word, he was a perfect gentleman. Mary had to spend much of what she earned on clothes, but it didn't seem to matter, since the bank was no longer pressing Mr. O for the house payments and he had found a job mucking stables for a livery north of town. The job didn't pay enough to cover all of the house payments, but it put food on the table and allowed Mr. O, with help from Mary, to pay two out of three payments when due.

Trent expanded his courting to include lunches and Mary packed the picnic lunches. Each day he picked her up at Hawshorn's store in a surrey, drove her home to pick up the picnic basket and then drove out to a secluded spot on the bay. They sat in the shade of a large weeping willow and talked about nothing important. Each time they sat under the willow, Trent sat a little closer to Mary. It was after their sixth lunch that he put his arm around Mary's waist. She didn't object, so he moved his face close to hers and gave her a peck on the cheek. She turned her head away.

THE CHINOOK RIVER PRINCESS

Trent was angry, "What's wrong with you? We've been seeing each other for almost a month now and you are still playing keep away?" He grabbed her under the jaw with his right hand and turned her face to his. Then he kissed her hard on the lips.

She tried to pull away, but he pushed her back onto the grass and slid his right hand into her bodice and over her left breast. She put her right hand on his chest and tried to push him up, but his weight was too much for her. She bit his upper lip until she tasted the salt of his blood.

"Bitch!" He sat up abruptly and ran the tip of his tongue across his cut lip..

"I thought you were supposed to be a perfect gentleman."

"Just how long did you think I would have the bank carry the Olsens without some kind of compensation?"

"You said just dinner and conversation."

"There comes a time in a courtship when dinner and conversation isn't enough."

Mary got quickly to her feet, then bent over and started tossing the utensils and leftovers into the basket.

"What do you think you're doing?" Trent got to his feet.

"I'm packing up to go home."

"The hell you are!" He grabbed her by the arm and pulled her close.

Mary drew her leg back and let it fly, trying to kick him in the kneecap. She missed and caught him full in the groin. He grabbed his crotch as his eyes rolled back, just before he toppled onto his side.

Mary finished packing the basket and folding the table cloth she had set out. She saw Trent's eyes following her actions. "If you haven't guessed, the courtship has ended." Her voice was cold.

Mary found Sam that evening on the porch of the rickety shack that was his home. He was rocking gently in the hickory rocker he had made with his own hands and a whittling knife. Knowing Sam too well to feel obligated to exchange a ritual greeting, she climbed the weathered stairs without ceremony. She then turned and sat on the edge of the porch, with her feet resting on the next step down. She wrapped her arms around and under her legs, holding her full dress tight to her thighs. After a few moments' silence, she told him that she was considering Father O'Brien's proposal again. Sam suppressed his elation.

Like Father O'Brien, Sam's own feelings colored his judgment. In his eyes, the people of Baltimore had grown slovenly in their opulence, no longer toiling as they had when the city was young and struggling for survival. The town folks' eyes had lost the gleam that comes from winning the daily contests of life. They moved in the same manner day after day, with ships coming and going and cargos loaded and unloaded. The harbor town was no longer stimulated by the new, the untried, or the untested; it was plagued by the old and mundane.

Sam could visualize Mary growing old in Baltimore, from boredom and lack of stimulation. Like the Padre, Sam had reached that time of life when a man, in quiet desperation, questions everything around him and craves the opportunity for stimulating experience.

"Miss Mary, mebe y'oughta go. T'aint nothin to keep ya here, an' out there ya might make a life for yo'self."

"What kind of a life?"

"A good un, Missy. Ma life here's a mite betta than t'was a slave, but notta ho' lot. Iffin I wuz working the land, I'd be a mite betta than now. Thar no way I kin git a piece o'land for m'sef, but dat's what'd do me happy. When I's worked the soil it was good. Now I jus' make casks go from over heah to over theah." He pointed from one end of the porch to the other, seeing the warehouse that was permanently etched into his consciousness. "Times I feels like maybe bin betta dat swamp-gater shudda got me."

"Don't you say that!" Mary scolded. "Don't you ever say that again! You're all I have left in the world and if you weren't here, I don't know what I'd do."

"Zat it, Miss Mary?" He turned his head slightly to the side and looked at her through a squinty left eye. "You won't go cause ya don' wan ta leave ol' Sam heah?"

"Don't be silly, that's not why I don't want to go... because if I went, I'd want you to go with me." Mary laid her head on her knees and turned it so she could see his reaction. His rocker's unvarying rhythm didn't reveal his emotion; it was betrayed by the shiny streaks that suddenly appeared on his ebony cheeks.

"Mr. March has a lot of land, I understand, and I bet there would be a lot of work to do there." She thought that Sam's last chance for happiness in a world not made for freed blacks might rest in her hands.

"Ya don' wanna leave Bal'mer." He stated her forgotten oath of only days before.

"Of course I do, but only if you take me."

"D'ya means it? Ya fur certain means it?" he asked without taking a breath. He leaned forward in his chair to hear her answer.

"I mean it. I want you to take me west, to my new home." She almost choked on her words, realizing as she uttered them that she would marry a total stranger.

"Oh Lord 'bove!" Sam sat upright in his chair again and stared toward the horizon at nothing in particular. "We's goin' west."

"We sure are," Mary got to her feet. She moved behind him and, reaching over the back of his rustic chair, hugged his enormous wooly head as she'd hug a large friendly dog.

Mary told Father O'Brien to write John March right away, telling him that she would go to Idaho to become Mrs. March as soon as he sent a bank check for two thousand dollars to the Bank of Baltimore in her name.

It was only five weeks after Father O'Brien posted his letter that Trent Kirby burst into Mr. Hawshorn's pipe shop. "Mary, what's the meaning of the check we received from a bank in Boise made out to you?"

"Oh, it came already?"

"Who's it from?"

"It's from my future husband, John March. It's to pay off the loan on the Olsens' house and for my trip west."

"What do you mean, future husband?"

"I'm going west to marry Mr. John March, who owns a very large ranch in Idaho."

"Forget it, the bank won't honor it!" He turned and marched out of the store.

THE CHINOOK RIVER PRINCESS

Mr. Hawshorn came into the store through the doorway to his shop. "I heard, Mary."

"Can he do that, Mr. Hawshorn?"

"No, not as long as I'm breathing he can't. Let's go to the police station, Lieutenant Henderson is a good friend of mine, a pipe smoker from way back."

Mary, Mr. Hawshorn, and Lieutenant Henderson stood in front of Trent Kirby's desk.

"I understand that you have a check for Miss Mary Harper here." The lieutenant's voice was hard.

"Where did you hear that?" Trent tried to act surprised but failed.

"From right here," Mr. Hawshorn stepped forward. "I heard everything from my shop."

"Well, what of it?"

The lieutenant made it clear that he wasn't going to play Trent's games. "Are you going to cash it, or will she have to take it to another bank?"

"We'll cash it, of course." Trent reached into his desk drawer, removed the check, then called to the closest teller, "Mr. Broom, please cash this check for Miss Harper."

Mary quickly spoke up. "I would like to use some of the money to pay off the loan on the Olsen house."

"Oh, there's isn't enough to do that," Trent objected.

"Mr. Olsen said he owed about thirteen hundred dollars on the loan over a month ago."

"I'm sure he's mistaken, Miss Harper."

"Let me see your records of the loan, Mr. Kirby." The lieutenant put his hand out.

"Our loan records are private."

"You produce the records right now, or the next time I see your little brother spit on the walk in front of Walton's Candy Store, I'll throw him in a cell with the drunken sailors and keep him there until Judge Samuels gets back in town."

Trent flushed crimson. "Mr. Broom, when you finish getting the cash for Miss Harper's check, get the loan ledger for the Olsen house."

The teller seemed to enjoy seeing Trent squirm. "Yes, Sir, Mr. Kirby."

Fifteen minutes later, when the three stepped onto the walk in front of the bank, Mary had a handful of cash. She had more money than she'd ever seen at one time, seven hundred and twenty-seven dollars, the balance of her check after paying off the loan on the Olsen house.

* * *

Baltimore was a bustling city throughout the nineteenth century, but it was especially busy in the year 1830, the hundredth anniversary of its founding. The city grew more exuberant every day as Founder's Day approached. All of the store and business owners had ordered special anniversary paraphernalia which was on display and were busy planning the big celebration. There was to be a parade through the center of town and it seemed that everyone was to give a speech extolling the virtues of Baltimore. After dark there was to be a grand display of fireworks. The special rockets and noisy firecrackers had been shipped in from Shanghai.

The approaching celebration was totally unimportant to Sam and Mary as they made plans for life in a new

THE CHINOOK RIVER PRINCESS

world. Celebrating the old was not on their list of priorities. It was purely coincidental that the day they chose to leave was Founder's Day, October 11, 1830. As Mary and Sam made their way through the throng of celebrants, Mary could not help imagining that the jubilee was to honor their journey.

Sam pushed a handcart ahead of him toward the railroad station and Mary walked at his side. The cart held five suitcases of hers, which were filled with everything dear to her. The cart held only one large carpetbag of his. In addition to her five suitcases, the cart carried the ship's footlocker Mary inherited from her father. It was packed with the few things that linked her past to the present: her father's blue waistcoat, three of her mother's dresses, her mother's hairbrushes, a ceramic pitcher her father bought her mother in London, several tea cups of unknown origin, a music box that belonged to her long departed grandmother and, of course, the beautiful pipe she bought for her father's birthday. Mrs. O had helped her fill the sea chest and move it to the Olsen house before the auction.

When the train pulled out of the station, Mrs. O was there, waving good-bye. Mary waved vigorously until Mrs. O disappeared around a bend as the tracks gradually turned. The tracks paralleled Main Street for about a mile and Mary saw the parade moving toward the center of the city. Through the coal-smoked window of the railroad car, Mary watched the civilized part of America pass by. The steam locomotive chugged its way across the Appalachians, which were a symphony of color that October day. They saw small towns, villages and farms on their way to Saint Louis, the jumping off place.

Chapter 8

In Saint Louis Sam got a job as a blacksmith's helper and Mary worked waiting tables in a hotel restaurant. They lived in a two-room tenement near the river until the ice broke in the spring.

"I thinks it's time ta finds a wagon train, Miss Mary," Sam said one evening. "Ice 'bout gone now an river boat's 'bout due. Wagon trains be startin' soon 'nuff I 'spect."

"You're right. At the hotel I overheard three men talking about joining a wagon train. They seemed to think a man named Adam Powder was the best Wagon master in St. Louis."

The next afternoon, Mary and Sam walked into the Center Street Saloon at the edge of town, near the river docks. As soon as they entered, the banter died; everyone looked their way. The room smelled of stale beer, clothes that had gone too long unwashed, and stale tobacco smoke. The dust in the air sparkled in the sunlight that came though the window at the far end of the room.

"We're looking for Mr. Powder," Mary tried to sound worldly. "We understand he often frequents this establishment."

"Frequents this establishment?" A man slouched at a table guffawed. "If that means passes out in the center of the floor, dead drunk, you're right." Several others laughed.

THE CHINOOK RIVER PRINCESS

"We want to talk to him about joining a wagon train."

"Who doesn't?" a man at the bar cracked, without turning around.

"Where can we find him?"

"He's upstairs, still asleep I expect," the man at the table offered. "He doesn't get up before two or three this early in the season."

"Can we wake him?"

"Sure, lady. Just go up to the second room from the top of the stairs and wake him."

"Thank you," Mary said before turning to join Sam, who had already started climbing the stairs.

The man at the table and several at the bar laughed and shook their heads.

Mary knocked on the door and Sam stood behind her. She knocked three times before they heard movement inside.

"What the hell is it?"

"Mr. Powder?" Mary had to shout at the door frame.

"What do you want?"

"I want to talk to you about joining your train going west."

"It's too early."

"I can come back."

"Do that—in about two weeks."

"That's too late. I need to start making plans now."

"What kind of plans?"

"I need to know what to buy for the trip."

"Do you have a wagon and team?"

"No."

"Go see Dan Geraard at the Wagon's West supply yard at the other end of town. Tell'em I sent ya. He'll fix you up with all you'll need. Don't let him talk you into any mules; you want a team of oxen."

"That's all?"

"He knows everything I require for my wagons. He'll try to sell you twice as much as you need, so buy half of everything he says you'll need. How many will be in your wagon?"

"Just two of us."

"Only one barrel of flour and one barrel of salt bacon."

"Thank you, Mr. Powder," Mary shouted, leaning against the door frame.

The Wagon's West sales building was a monstrous warehouse. It was painted apple green and stood across the street from the Teams West stockyard for harness animals.

They entered the front door and Sam said, "Smells laik da shipyard back 'ome; fresh split oak."

"Look at all the wagons." Mary said. "There must be fifty."

"Sixty-two." The voice came from her left. "We have any wagon you could ever want. I'm Dan Geraard." The salesman put out his hand, but Mary ignored it.

"We don't know what we want. Mr. Powder sent us. I'm Mary Harper and this is my traveling companion, Sam Grande."

"How far are you going?"

"The Chinook River. Idaho."

"That's a long way. I would recommend a heavy wagon like this one," he said, walking over to a massive

THE CHINOOK RIVER PRINCESS

bright green wagon with five-foot, ten-spoke wheels in the rear and four-foot, six-spoke wheels in the front.

"That's awfully big. There are only the two of us and we don't have any furniture."

"No furniture? No beds?"

"No beds."

"Not even a chest of drawers?"

"No furniture."

"You planning on eating and sleeping on the floor when you're there?"

"I'm going to join my husband. The house is already furnished."

"Oh. I still recommend this big wagon here. It's made strong. The wheels won't collapse when you hit a big rock the wrong way and it will float the Platt and the other rivers when they're high. The smaller wagons'll sink like stones."

"How much does it cost?"

"That depends."

"Depends on what?"

"Well, I can make you a deal if you're going to let me stock it for you. If you're going to buy your provisions elsewhere the price will be higher."

"How much if we let you stock it?"

"Depends?"

"On what now?"

"On how much provisions you need."

"We just need enough for the two of us."

"Well, then this is what you'll need." He pulled a list from his shirt pocket. "Hardware... you'll need: a pickaxe, two shovels, a wagon tool kit—"

"A tool kit doesn't come with the wagon?" Mary wanted to make it clear that she wasn't a pushover.

"No. Tool kit's extra. Five hundred feet of three-quarter inch hemp rope, a full length ax, a hatchet, a two-pound wooden mallet, five extra spokes, two extra wheel rims, a small anvil an iron hammer, ten pounds of axle grease, a fifty-pound keg of nails—"

"What are the nails for?"

"Oh, that's right. You won't be needing the nails. That's for people setting up a new homestead. Two twenty-foot oak pry poles to lift the wagon when you need to take off a wheel for greasing, a set of campfire cookware, a large kettle, a meat cleaver, a set of various sized carving knives with two sharpening stones, a campfire tripod stand for the kettle, and a Dutch oven for baking bread. For food, you'll need two barrels of flour, two barrels of bacon—"

"The list says one barrel of flour and one barrel of bacon," Mary was now standing beside Geraard and pointing to the paper.

"That's for one adult. You have to double it for two adults, especially because your nigger here looks like he eats for two normal sized men."

"Well I eat like a bird so we'll be only needing what's on the list and my man here is Sam Grande. I would appreciate your addressing him as Mr. Grande."

"As you wish, Ma'am. You'll also need a keg of corn meal, a keg of dried beef, two fifty-pound sacks of dried beans, twenty pounds of salt, ten salt licks for the mules—"

"Oxen, Mr. Geraard."

"Mules are your best bet, Ma'am. They move faster than oxen and you take an extra two just in case a few die. You can ride the extras when you get tired of walking or riding on the wagon seat. You don't ride oxen."

"I want oxen."

"Oxen are a bit more expensive, too."

"Oxen, Mr. Geraard."

"Fine, Oxen it is. You'll need a keg of sugar, a five-pound tin of soda, twenty pounds of soap and all the regular spices."

"How much for everything—the wagon, oxen, hardware, and provisions?"

"Well, let me just add it up."

"Don't bother. You know exactly what it is."

He smiled with tight lips for just a moment. "It will be nine hundred and fifty dollars for everything."

"Seven-fifty," she countered.

"Seven-fifty?"

"Seven-fifty or I go back down the street to the wagon shop we passed coming here."

"You drive a hard bargain."

"It's early in the season and you don't have any other customers. The way I figure it, you need the cash and if you don't, the other wagon shop probably does."

"Eight hundred," Geraard countered.

"Okay, be that way. Seven-forty," Mary didn't try to hide her anger.

"Okay, seven-fifty cash... and right away not when you pick up the wagon."

"Fine." Mary opened her purse and pulled out a wad of bills. She handed over the entire wad.

He counted it as exactly seven hundred fifty dollars. "That's all you had."

"That's right."

"It's a pleasure taking all your money, Ma'am."

"We'll be back in a couple of weeks and everything had better be ready and nothing had better be missing."

When they got outside Sam looked panicked.. "Dat alls the money, Miss Mary?"

"No, Sam. That's all the money I was willing to spend. A number of men at the hotel told me not to spend more that eight hundred for everything."

"Wheres da rest?"

"In the top of my boot, Sam."

"Yo pappy'd be prouds a you, Miss Mary." He smiled broadly.

Chapter 9

The heat was stifling. Mary could hardly see the horizon through the shimmering heat waves. The underarms of her dress were a reddish brown from the trail dust that stuck to the sweat-soaked cotton. Perspiration rolled out from under her bonnet and seeped under the back of her collar.

As she walked through the tall grass beside the wagon, she tried to imagine what her new home would be like. She had no experience to draw upon and no picture came to mind. Just as she had no experience to imagine her new home, nothing could have prepared her for the impact of the plains. Back east she had never been able to see a distance of more than a few miles. Her view was always obstructed by trees, buildings, and the rolling terrain. Here there was nothing but grass as far as she could see, and she could see about forty miles whenever the train of wagons broached a rise in the terrain.

Mary was almost overcome with anxiety when the wagons first entered the vast plains. The sky occupied most of her field of view and it was oppressively immense. She felt as if she were an ant standing on an immense, flat, grass-covered plate that was rising into the heavens. The expanse of blue stretched around her in all directions. At times she looked up at the massive blue canopy overhead as she walked and grew dizzy. When each such dizzy spell passed, she was left breathless with anxiety. She feared that she wouldn't be able to adjust to her new home if it were as vast as the rolling grasslands.

Theirs was the next to last wagon of the ten-wagon train, and Sam drove the team. Mary strode tirelessly behind the wagon, or beside Sarah, the more lazy of the two oxen. Standing next to Sarah, she could smack the huge beast on the flank with a stout stick when the old girl needed motivation.

The trail was well worn. Thousands of wagons had made the arduous journey over the years since men had first been inspired to move their families west. When the first wagons rolled over the plains there had been no trail. There had been only grass—an unbroken tapestry of greens and browns.

In the very early days of the expansion the greatest obstacle had been monotony, but now that the wagons were bound to the wheel-worn trail, the adversity that surpassed even the monotony was dust. The wheel ruts were filled with as much as six inches of powder—dust so fine that once airborne, it could penetrate any luggage or sealed box.

Mary, the other women, and the children, walked rather than rode on the wagons. They walked in order to avoid the choking dust. When there was a breeze, those on foot walked on the windward side of the train. When the air was still, they walked as much as a quarter mile to the left or right of the trail to avoid the standing cloud that engulfed the wagons. Only the first wagon avoided the dust, having only to contend with that kicked up by its own team. The wagons rotated turns in the coveted lead position. The trail had become so crowded in recent years that even being the first in the train didn't assure a

THE CHINOOK RIVER PRINCESS

relatively dust free ride. Some days, the trail was filled with trains of wagons, nose-to-tailgate, stretching from horizon to horizon.

Sam wore a bandanna tied across his face. Only tiny slits showed where his eyes peered out from under the wide beaver-felt hat he wore down low over his brow. Even so covered, his eyelashes were encrusted with mud that formed from the irritating dust and the futile tears it constantly drew forth.

Just after the sun passed its zenith, the air started to move. A gentle breeze blew directly at the front of the train. Their wagon was second from the front and Mary walked on the left side, about twenty yards from the wagon. Sometimes the wind shifted enough so that it pushed the dust where she walked. Mary picked up her pace and moved up parallel with the lead wagon, where the dust couldn't possibly get to her.

She reminisced about her life when both her mother and father were alive. She thought about the cool waters of the Chesapeake and remembered how it felt on her feet when she dangled them in the water off the edge of the dock.

There were nine other wagons, besides Mary's and Sam's. Two wagons carried newly wedded couples. The other seven carried families of from four to seven members. The wagon now in the lead bore the seven-member Stern family from Illinois. Jacob was the Stern's eldest son. He had blond hair, a simple Roman nose, and a wide and unashamed smile. His face was narrow, with high cheek bones and deep set eyes. His skin was as dark as a pecan shell and already wrinkled from the harsh sun he sat in day after day. His hands were large and hard and held the reins skillfully. His shirt sleeves were rolled up past his elbows and his forearms were as muscular as a colt's hindquarters. He looked much older than his nineteen years.

"This is the first time I've seen you so far from your wagon, Miss Harper."

Mary woke from her daydream with a start. She had been so lost in her thoughts that she had drifted within ten feet of the lead wagon. "Oh, Jacob," she said in surprise, looking up at the driver on the wagon seat. "I didn't realize where I was."

"It must have been some mighty pleasant thoughts you were having. I've been watching you. You've smiled more in the last quarter hour than you've smiled since we left Saint Louis."

Mary's face turned a bright crimson at the realization that he had been watching her. She tried to remember if she had done something unladylike without thinking. Her bloomers were forever working themselves between the cheeks of her derriere as she walked, and sometimes she grabbed them with a handful of her dress and pulled them to a more comfortable position. She couldn't remember anything about the previous half-hour walk much less whether she had been pulling at her bloomers.

"I was just thinking about the Chesapeake Bay back home."

"I've never seen the ocean or a bay." His tone was wistful.

"When I was a little girl, I loved the sea. I used to sit on the docks and watch the gulls glide overhead and listen to the waves slapping against the pilings."

"What are pilings?"

"Well," Mary was momentarily, caught off guard by his question, "a piling is like a long post that's out in the water and it goes all the way down into the ground under the water. A bunch of them are what hold up the dock or pier."

"What's a pier?"

"It's a long dock."

"Oh," Jacob looked confused, "I wish I could see the ocean. What's it look like?"

"It's blue and it goes as far as you can see." She looked out across the expanse of prairie, and pointed at the horizon. "Look out there and imagine that all the grass you see is water, and that it's all the same level, except there are waves or bumps on the water about two or three feet high, and there are troughs between the waves, just about as deep. Imagine that the waves rise and fall, turning from waves into troughs and then back again."

Jacob stared across the expanse of grass for about ten seconds. "I can't imagine it. I guess I'm too used to seeing land. What color blue is it? Light blue, dark blue?"

"It's all colors of blue. When the sun is bright and the sky is clear, it's a bright blue, like the sky just before sunset. When the sky is full of clouds it's kind of an oily blue-gray. In the morning about sunrise, it's a blue-black."

"It sounds kind of scary to me." Jacob shook his head.

"I never thought so, until my father was killed on a ship in a storm out there on the ocean."

"I'm sorry." The last thing he wanted was to upset her.

"It can be dangerous," she continued, without hearing what he said. "After he died, the ocean looked different to me. Before that I thought it was only good. It provided all kinds of fish for food, and boats sailed across it to other countries and brought back all kinds of marvelous things. After my father died, I saw that it could be evil. It looked different somehow, dangerous."

"I'd sure like to see it someday."

Mary walked silently along beside the wagon and Jacob continued to stare out across the seemingly endless expanse of green and brown grass. He rocked with the movement of the wagon as it slowly rolled and pitched in the deep, dust-filled ruts.

The next day, when his father was driving their wagon, Jacob offered to spell Sam on his and Mary's wagon. Sam had driven the team all but fifty or sixty miles of the trail since they left Saint Louis and was grateful for a chance to walk for a change. Jacob regularly spelled Sam after that; it gave him plenty of opportunity to talk to Mary.

When Jacob was driving, Mary walked on the windward side of the team, just ahead of the driver's seat. Jacob liked her to walk there, where he could watch her as he drove. Her spirit would soar whenever she glanced up and discovered that he was surveying her. The corners of his mouth turned up slightly whenever she looked his way but she quickly looked to the team whenever he started to smile. She didn't want to give reason for the rest of the train to start talking.

One evening after all had eaten their supper, which consisted primarily of beans, bacon, and soda-bread cooked over buffalo-chip fires, Mary strolled around the camp. As she walked, she heard the few literate fathers and mothers reading to their children from treasured family story books, or the family Bible. The open desolation of the prairie seemed to bring the family units closer. The children were eager to help their parents in order to gain their comforting praise. Parents were eager to help their children in order to gain a sense of accomplishment. All were eager to engage in activities which brought a feeling of security in the strange new environment.

As she passed the Stern family wagon, she heard Jacob's father telling his children a story. The whole family was sitting close to the smoldering, smoky fire. The story was about how Mr. Stern had earned enough money by working for a smith in a small town south of Chicago to buy his first piece of land. As Mary ambled past, Jacob excused himself and walked quickly to catch up with her.

"Evening, Mary." He looked straight ahead as he matched her strides.

"Good evening, Jacob." She tried to mask her emotion. Her heart had jumped to her throat when she heard his approaching footsteps.

"Pa says that we'll be gettin' to the mountains in about two months."

She sighed loudly. "I don't know if I can wait that long. I've had just about as much of this dust and grass and sky as I can stand."

"Yeah." He laughed lightly. "I'd give five dollars just to see a tree right now."

"I feel like there's nowhere I can go to be alone," Mary almost sobbed. "I can't even have any privacy. We women have to hide behind each other's skirts to do our daily duties."

"I know," he was nervous and highly embarrassed by Mary's remark, "mother says that's why the women on trains wear full skirts rather than pants."

"There is another reason, Jacob."

"What's that?"

"It would be easier for the women to wear pants but they want their husbands to know that they aren't going to work like hired hands when they get to their new homes. We wear these awful hot dresses to remind you men that we are ladies."

"You don't need a dress to remind me of that." There was a slight quaver in his voice.

"You mean that being out here in this desolate nowhere, gathering buffalo dung for the fire, hasn't hurt my delicate image?"

"I. . ." He started to say something but stopped. He had to muster courage before he blurted, "I think you are the prettiest lady that I ever seen."

Mary's blush went unnoticed in the fading evening light.

As they ambled aimlessly Mary wondered what it would be like to have the strong, quiet man make love to her. As she thought about it, a flush of warmth passed over her. She felt as though she were standing in the warmth that emanated from the stove in Mrs. Olsen's parlor on a winter evening. She couldn't resist taking Jacob's hand in hers.

Her action brought his feelings bubbling to the surface. He pulled her hand to him and then behind him so she was facing him with her arm held firmly around his lower

THE CHINOOK RIVER PRINCESS

back. In the darkness she could not see his face clearly, but she knew that it was filled with desire. She had no inclination to resist when he kissed her hard. She kissed him back. It was only a few feverish moments before she no longer could claim innocence. Even though it was a physically painful experience, it was as emotionally liberating as it was uplifting.

She lay under Jacob, looking at the canopy of stars over his shoulder. She was a changed person. From that moment on, the grass, the dust, the bright blue ceiling of day and the star-studded midnight-blue canopy of night became integral pieces of her happiness. At that moment, the harsh environment of the western frontier was as comforting as her feather bed had been back in Baltimore.

From the moment of their joining, Jacob and Mary had experienced a mutual life-long commitment of spirit and each knew that they would spend the rest of their lives as husband and wife. It was obvious also to the rest of the members of the train, who gave deference to their unenviable predicament.

Chapter 10

Mary and Jacob were totally and irrevocably in love but without the services of a pastor, could not finalize their commitment in public ceremony. Wagon master Powder offered to wed the two, but Mary's upbringing wouldn't allow for a non-religious union.

The members of the train refrained from watching the spiritual newlyweds and seemed not to notice their late-evening forays into the darkness beyond the perimeter of flickering light from the campfires. Every evening as the families entertained themselves with tales of folklore and performed the small tasks that could only be performed when the train was immobile, Mary and Jacob talked of the life that they would wrest from the wilderness. The two sat hand-in-hand near the smoldering buffalo-chip fire in straight-back chairs brought out of the wagons each evening. They spoke of the life they imagined awaited them and of the experiences that had made them uniquely themselves.

"I wonder if we'll be attacked by Indians before we get to the mountains?" Jacob queried as much to himself as to Mary one evening as the smoke from their fire drifted to the north on a slight breeze.

"Do they attack wagon trains very often?" Mary's concern grew.

"No. Not anymore. Years ago they did, but that was before there were so many trains and wagons in each train. They've lost too many men to our rifles."

"I couldn't kill another person." Mary was adamant.

"You could, given sufficient reason."

"Never!" Mary said vehemently.

"Oh yes, if the price of letting him live were too great."

"What are your saying, Jacob?"

"I think anyone would kill if he were protecting his child, or spouse, or home. I believe that there is a situation in which everyone could kill another. It is man's nature; only God can resist all temptation. Man can be very strong in his conviction and do what is right in most situations, but not all. Man is fallible, and that is what life is about."

"That's not what life's about, that what damnation is about."

"It is and it isn't. Mark my words, Mary. Under the right—or, if you prefer— wrong conditions, even you could kill another."

"I don't believe so, Jacob."

"I hope, for your sake, that you never have to find out."

"Amen to that," Mary was happy they found something to agree upon.

Sam had not expressed an opinion about what had developed between the young lovers, but he was not pleased. He had been a necessary piece of Mary's new life in the west, but he had now changed from being Mary's only family to being a tag-along.

Late one afternoon Sam brought up the subject of his future as Jacob watched Mary bake hard biscuits in a frying pan over the small fire. "I thinks I be findin' work on da coast whens we be done wid dis train."

"What?" Mary glanced quickly over her shoulder from her squatting position. "I thought we were going to stay together."

"I doan see da'd be good," He sat on a small stool at the rear of the wagon mending a harness that had worn almost through. "Youse gonna hafta work ta git nuff vittles off a homestead ta feeds yo'selfs."

"Don't be silly." Mary's reply was only halfhearted. He was right. She had known that John March had a large enough spread to support another hard working hand and had perceived Sam's presence as a blessing. He would have been an asset to the ranch as well as a good friend, but his presence would be a burden to her and Jacob as a newly married couple trying to make a go of a small farm. "I'll not stand in your way, Sam, if you want to go off on your own, but I wish you'd stay."

Mary expected Jacob to extend an offer of welcome to Sam also, but none came. Jacob, like Sam, had already concluded that a small homestead farm couldn't support the three of them.

Sam spoke with conviction. "I'll keeps movin' ta da coast."

"What will you do to earn a living?" Mary couldn't curb her curiosity.

"Thar's always docks where a bull the likes a me can gets work; doan fret 'bout dat."

Mary dropped the subject, feeling that she had done the right thing by asking Sam to stay but knowing that it was best, under the circumstances, that he didn't.

THE CHINOOK RIVER PRINCESS

The Bosch family from Massachusetts, were one of the happier groups in the train. Heinrich Bosch had come to New York from Germany in 1810, when he was twenty. He tried to find work in the city but there were too many new Europeans for the number of jobs. He heard that the mills were hiring up north, so he walked and begged his way to Boston. It was there that he finally found steady work and met his future wife, Gurt. She was also German and the two were naturally drawn together. They both loved children and before they knew it, they had three.

In the old country, Heinrich's father had a herd of dairy cows and made some of the finest cheese and Heinrich missed the rural atmosphere and the honest labor of farm life. He couldn't imagine spending the remainder of his days fixing shuttle cocks for the looms. Luckily, Gurt didn't appreciate the urban life any more than Heinrich; she couldn't see herself doing laundry for the other tenants in their building when she was an old woman. She agreed that they should save as much of their earnings as possible and buy a farm west of the Mississippi.

It took them only five years to save seventeen hundred dollars, enough to buy passage to St. Louis, buy and provision a large wagon, and have about four hundred left over to buy a farm. Over those five years, they managed to have three more children—six in all—ranging from age three to fifteen.

The Bosch clan was a loving and happy one and Mary smiled whenever she passed their wagon. It was the littlest Bosch, with the tongue-twisting name of Josh, who caught Mary's eye. Mary thought it cruel that they would saddle a child with a name so hard to say as Josh Bosch.

Josh was always giggling and running close to his sisters and brothers, trying to get one to chase him. Once in a while, one of the other Bosch children would humor him by chasing him around the campsite while he screamed bloody murder. The chase continued until he was caught and tickled unmercifully—he loved being tickled.

One evening as Mary and Jacob were walking around the camp exchanging greetings with the various families, Josh ran close to Mary and stopped. He turned, faced Mary, and grinned. He turned his back again as if ready to run and looked back over his shoulder to see if Mary would chase him. Mary just stomped her feet quickly in the dirt and Josh screamed and took off running through the camp. When he realized Mary wasn't chasing him, he circled back and taunted her again. Again Mary stomped her feet, but Josh only ran a few steps before looking back and stopping. Mary tried stomping her feet once more, but he just stood firm and put his hands on his hips in a very grown-up gesture of disgust. It must have been something his father did.

Mary then took off running after Josh and his eyes grew very large. He turned and tried to run but his overconfidence had caused his undoing. Mary picked him up by the waist and lifted him high in the air as he squealed with delight. Then Mary set him back down on the ground and tickled his sides as he giggled incessantly. Mary finally patted him on the bottom and sent him scurrying back to the Bosch's campfire. Josh's brothers and sisters all laughed and waved to Mary as she walked back to join Jacob. From that night on, it was Mary's evening duty to chase Josh, at least a few times, around

THE CHINOOK RIVER PRINCESS

the camp and to tickle him into submission. Mary grew exceptionally fond of Josh and it was obvious he felt the same way about her.

Sometimes Josh would walk with his mother and Mary as the wagons ambled west. He walked between the two women with his arms held high, holding their hands. He would look from his mother to Mary and back again and grin. He was the happiest little boy Mary had ever met.

One evening as Jacob and Mary ambled around the camp on their regular walk, Josh ran up to Mary and put his arms in the air. Mary picked him up and set him to straddle her hip.

"Chase me?" He tipped his head to the side in a cute gesture.

"Not right now, dear. Jacob and I are on a walk. Maybe in a little later."

"Okay." Josh smiled and pushed gently on Mary's shoulder to let her know he wanted to be put down.

Mary set him on the ground and he went back to the Bosch campfire. Jacob and Mary continued to walk until they were beyond the reach of the light of the campfires. They sat in the tall prairie grass and held each other tightly. Then they kissed
until that didn't seem enough and finally made love in their ritual fashion, with Mary's many petticoats providing little cushion. As they were walking back toward the camp, they heard an unholy wail, a high-pitched sorrowful note that continued for almost twenty seconds before a second wail joined the first.

Mary and Jacob began running and when they reached the camp there was a crowd beside the Conner's wagon—the source of the awful wailing. Jacob and Mary worked their way through the tight mass of people until they could see what had engrossed everyone.

Mr. and Mrs. Bosch were on their knees rocking forward and back, holding their heads and sobbing. Between them, in his miniature blue-plaid shirt and dark blue cotton pants, was Josh. He wasn't laughing or giggling or running and playing; he was lying perfectly still with his arms at his sides, so unlike him. Mary pushed several big men aside and stood over the site. Josh looked very serene and peaceful, as if he were sleeping. A quarter-circle red line crossed the middle of his forehead, came down the left side of the bridge of his tiny nose and across his left cheek. There was blood oozing from the line and Mary saw that Josh's forehead and cheek were sunken in a little.

"Wh...what happened?" Mary stammered.

"The little boy walked behind Mr. Conner's mules tethered beside the wagon. I guess he spooked one and it just flicked his hoof like he was shooing a horsefly. . . caught him in the face."

"Will he be all right?"

"He's dead, Miss Harper."

As the stars moved across the heavens overhead, Mary and Mrs. Conners helped prepare little Josh for burial to spare Josh's family. The two women washed the blood from his face and left ear and combed his light brown hair. They wrapped him in clean blanket, his little arms around his favorite rag horse. Tears ran down Mary's cheeks in rivulets and fell off her chin in a steady dripping stream. She didn't make a sound but her shoulders often shook and her head fell forward, her chin on her chest.

THE CHINOOK RIVER PRINCESS

They didn't have spare wood for a coffin, so Sam tore every other board from the bed of their wagon. He worked by the light of an oil lamp, making a small but tight box, like the wrights he watched in Baltimore had built ships. He even hammered paraffin-soaked cotton rags between the wooden slats, to make Josh's little soul ship watertight.

Sam's mother had told him when he was a little boy on the Grande plantation, that back home across the large water, their people put loved ones in boats and sailed them down river, beyond the edge of their world, to join their gods and their ancestors. He had seen how much joy the little boy had brought Mary. Sam had to be sure the little fellow would make it all the way back to his gods and his loving ancestors. Josh was being sent off with plenty of water to sail on—not only was his blanket wet with Mary's tears, but his little boat almost needed bailing because of Sam's tears. By the light of the half moon, Sam dug a very deep hole as the Coyotes howled a soulful tune.

At sunrise everyone joined the Bosch family at the grave site. A family Bible was passed among the mourners and those who could, read a passage. Mary tried but could only blubber so Sam took the book and passed it to Jacob, who read about Jesus and the little children. The Bible would have been passed forever if Mr. Bosch had not stepped in and said, "It's enough; we must say *auweidersein* now."

Mrs. Bosch started wailing more loudly then; it meant she would soon be separated from her little Josh.

Mr. Bosch and his other children pressed in close and held Mrs. Bosch tightly as Sam and Jacob lowered Josh's small boat down into the deep, shade-filled hole with two hemp ropes. Mary thought it cruel that it was such a beautiful morning. The sky was golden from the sliver of sun that peeked over the grassy hill. The golden light lit up only the top two inches of the western lip of the grave. Mary was devastated to see the coffin drop into the harsh darkness below the edge of the sharp-cut sod.

The men climbed onto the wagon seats and started the wagons moving, while the women and children walked en mass slowly beside them. One of the older boys from another wagon, without being asked, climbed up onto the seat of Mary's and Sam's wagon and drove it with the others.

When the train was out of ear shot, Sam and Jacob started shoveling the earth back in the hole. There was a kind of simple rhythmic music as the small rocks bounced off the lid.

Sam was crying again as he hammered the little wooden cross at the head of the grave. Jacob picked up the shovels and started walking quickly to catch up with the wagons.

The archangel of light was just behind Sam as he hammered the final strokes.

The dark angel appeared at her side with a concerned look. "What are you doing here? This has nothing to do with the ring, does it?"

"No, but then again, it does. You wouldn't understand."

"So tell me. What is it that has to do with the ring?"

"It's this man's crying over the soul of another."

"What's so special about that? People always cry over lost loved ones."

"Ah yes, but this man cries over someone he knows but only a little."

"I don't understand."

"No, you don't, and never will." She winked out the way she had come.

The dark angel glanced sideways at Sam and furrowed his scaly brow a moment before he vanished.

Chapter 11

The rest of that day, Mary studied the grave markers along the trail. "There are so many." Sam looked at her hands which she wrung together as the wagon rocked on the uneven dusty roadway.

"Theys been right many right along, Miss Mary."

"I guess I saw them but never really thought about them. I never saw them as beautiful little children. I assumed they were older men and women. Men who died fighting for their families or died of exhaustion; women who just wore out or died of the consumption. I never imagined innocent little children under those grave markers."

Sam didn't say anything; there wasn't anything to say. Mary pulled the hem of her dress up to her face and wiped her wet eyes. Sam's eyes were still glassy, as they had been all day.

"When will I stop crying, Sam?"

"Whens thar ain't no mo' chillen, I 'spects," he said tonelessly.

Mary bent forward at the waist and buried her face in the handfuls of dress she was holding at her knees. She wept loudly.

In the fifth month of their journey, as the terrain changed from flat plain to rolling foothills, the members of the train sighted the Devil's Pedestal. The cylindrical

THE CHINOOK RIVER PRINCESS

monolith rose over eight-hundred feet into the air and looked like nothing they had ever seen. The mass of stone was composed of a bundle of several thousand hexagonal basaltic cylinders several feet in diameter, that had crystallized inside the throat of a volcanic cone thousands of years before. It was the action of the wind and rain over countless cycles of seasons that had removed the outer cone of ash, leaving the core to stand as a lonely sentinel, a witness to the ceaseless march of time.

Native residents of the region believed that the vertical ridges in the monolith, which are actually the crystallized joints between the small cylinders, were the claw marks of bears that had tried to kill the young maidens of their clan in the time of their most distant forefathers. They knew because their fathers had told them, as had their fathers before them. The gods had raised the land upon which the maidens stood, in order to keep the maidens safe from bears. The bears had attacked as the maidens were picking berries for use by the tribal elders in holy ceremonies. The frustrated bears, as the story went, raked the sides of the raised land with their claws, as the gods lifted the maidens from the top of the holy pedestal.

Unlike the Indians, the newcomers had no idea what caused the unusual structure, and it was a sense of overwhelming curiosity that enticed trains of wagons to make camp at the base of the unusual rock tower.

Jacob was so impressed with the towering rock that he convinced Mary to accompany him on a hike through the sparse pines that surrounded the mysterious structure. Jacob said nothing to Mary but he felt compelled by divine entreaty to investigate the mysteries of the tower. He resisted at first but finally succumbed to the feeling that the object was a heaven-sent messenger of some sort and that he was the only one to receive the message.

As they climbed the slope of dirt and broken basaltic fingers that formed the approach to the towering pedestal, Mary began to feel the inspiration that assailed Jacob. While the pedestal was only impressive at a distance, it was overwhelming up close. To them, the perfect hexagonal cylinders, which joined each other within a tolerance of thousandths of an inch, were testaments to the deliberate nature of the holy creation.

The two climbed the loose material toward the tower as if possessed. They forced their way through the scrub brush that ringed the top of the slope. They were as children in their eagerness.

"Quickly! We're almost there!" Jacob had trouble speaking between gasps for air.

"I'm coming." She lifted her skirts high to clear the broken rock strewn in her path.

"Look!" He pointed to series of broken cylinders rising one behind the other, forming a staircase on the side of the rock mass.

"Don't!" Mary pleaded as Jacob bounded up the first and second cylindrical steps before the word had cleared her lips.

"Come on, Mary. How can you not?" He looked back only for a moment before continuing.

"Stop!" A dreadful apprehension washed over Mary. The ominous feeling was so overwhelming it made her nauseous. "Don't go any further!"

"What's wrong?" He was angry with her and stood twenty feet higher on the sixth pedestal of the unusual staircase. He stood perfectly still, staring up at the sky above, his hands extended down and out to his sides. "This was made for a reason. We're supposed to be here. It's written, I know it."

"I'm afraid, Jacob. Come down to me, please."

"Nonsense!" He then turned and vaulted each of the remaining twelve stones, each higher than the next, like the pipes of a church organ. As he stood on the last stair that marked the end of his ascent, only a fraction of the way up the side of the tower, he looked out over the rugged landscape and took a deep breath of the pine-perfumed air. He held his breath for a few moments before letting it escape between his smiling lips.

The sound of Jacob's exhalation was all that was needed to finally spook the nervous hawk that was nesting on a ledge just twelve feet above his head. Jacob watched the graceful feathered creature as it soared away, after swooping down to gain speed for its gliding departure. An instant later the small rock that the bird had dislodged from his nesting ledge, hit Jacob on the back of the head. It was only a small rock, but large enough that it surprised and unbalanced him on his restricted perch.

Jacob grasped for a handhold on the smooth rock cylinders as his fear-stiffened body slowly tilted away from the vertical stone face. In the endless moment of his first realization of what had befallen him, he recalled his fathers words when he had climbed to the very top of a tall oak on the farm ten years earlier. His father, who was wise beyond most other men, had said, "Never climb higher than you can afford to fall."

As he gained momentum in his descent, Jacob foolishly wondered if his father would be angry with him. Mary was too surprised to scream and involuntarily held her breath as Jacob's outstretched shape gracefully rotated three-quarters of a full turn in the air before slamming to the earth. He landed flat on his back. His head stopped abruptly as the base of his skull impacted on a flat section of rock that protruded only several inches from the surrounding soil.

Mary reached him before all the dust from his impact had settled. She stood motionlessly at his side. Her head seemed to pulsate with each beat of her heart. There was a sound in her ears which was more like a roar than a buzz. Jacob looked straight up at the rock face but his smashed brain registered nothing. She knelt beside his chest and, slipping one hand under his head and the other under his shoulder, tried to raise him to his feet. She struggled several seconds before starting to scream. She screamed when she realized that the back of his head was as soft as a cloth sack of cottage cheese. She screamed, just for a moment, before a merciful darkness washed over her.

An uneasy quiet hung over the train as the wagons rumbled further westward. Mary lay trance-like in her wagon, as Sam deftly guided the oxen with a firm hand.

It had happened again—Mary had lost what mattered most to her. Her mother, father, her home, and now her first love. What had she done? How much did she owe? As she lay in the dusty wagon, rocking violently as the wagon creaked and groaned over the uneven terrain, she tried to recall everything she had ever done in a desperate attempt to understand her torment.

As she stared up from her bed, she saw dust particles dancing through a shaft of light that streamed in from a

THE CHINOOK RIVER PRINCESS

small hole in the canvas cover. They reminded her of the snow that had fallen on the night that Muffin died.

Muffin was a kitten her father had given her when she was five years old. It was one of six that had been born to a cat on her father's ship. The cat had slipped ashore in Portugal one night and as a result, six little fur balls had been born in a makeshift nest behind the stove in the galley as the ship bobbed in rough seas off Iceland. Mary called the kitten Muffin because it smelled fresh and sweet, like the muffins that her mother made for Sunday morning breakfast.

One January evening, after her mother and father had tucked her in for the night with Muffin and kisses, she noticed a wet spot in the bed. She was almost as angry as she thought her mother would be. In a fit of anger, she pulled open the window, which was almost too much for her to handle, and placed Muffin on the widow's walk that extended around the roof just outside her bedroom.

It wasn't too cold at eight in the evening, but that night a wind from the northwest brought in arctic chill that hadn't been seen on the bay for ten years. She meant only to leave him out for a few minutes to teach him a lesson, but she quickly fell asleep. In the morning, she lay in bed upon waking, marveling at the pretty frost patterns that had formed on the window panes. She remembered Muffin and quickly ran to the window, which was frozen shut. After trying in vain to open it, she rubbed a hole in the frost and peered out to see Muffin's soft fur form lying lifelessly on the walk. She had murdered her little Muffin and that, she now concluded in her confused state, was what had brought the Lord's wrath upon her.

As the days passed, Sam grew more and more angry with the other members of the train. When all was well, they had been all too eager to revel in the young couple's happiness. Women had looked at each other and smiled in a knowing way at those countless times when Mary and Jacob had left the close company of the group to find privacy in the darkness beyond the flickering firelight. In so doing, the other members of the wagon train had tacitly approved of the unblessed relationship.

Now the women talked among themselves in hushed whispers, expressing their distaste for the way the young couple had acted—their distaste for the actions, which they now concluded, had caused the Lord's violent admonition. Each now claimed to have privately disapproved of the shameless actions. Sam, being a semi-illiterate emancipated slave, didn't know there was a word to describe their actions, but even so he recognized and resented their hypocrisy.

Sam grew angry with the members of the train who cast unapproving looks at Mary whenever they passed the wagon. The train had changed—it was no longer a close knit community offering support—it had become a judgmental mob. Sam knew it would be best for Mary if they struck out on their own, so as soon as they entered the flats along the upper Snake River, he turned their wagon northwest across the plateau. Slowly the distance grew and Sam put miles between Mary and the resentment of the others. For three days, his deft hands guided the oxen team across sixty miles of sandy sage-covered soil until they reached the scarp at the edge of the Snake River canyon. The wagon rocked and creaked along the narrow rutted trail that followed the canyon rim.

THE CHINOOK RIVER PRINCESS

The land was devoid of what easterners considered vegetation. The ground was a powdery gray clay, blanketed with sage, the only vegetation that could tolerate the scorching arid summer air.

The odor of sage was so strong it made Mary light-headed. She seemed to be in some kind of shock or denial, a state which protected her from thoughts of Jacob. Her face glowed with a childish innocence as she trod along in front of the team, as she rejoiced in all of the life she saw. She marveled at the little yellow hornets that swarmed around her feet as she trod among their nesting holes in the dirt. She smiled as she put her hand up to shade her eyes as she surveyed the falcons as they soared overhead, looking for small prey on the canyon walls below.

Chapter 12

Sam drove the wagon across a hundred and fifty miles of desert beside the Snake River and then turned the wagon east where the Snake River met the Chinook River. He then drove the wagon down the most gentle slope he could find, into the Chinook River Valley. The canyon walls rose three hundred feet over their heads. It was mid-summer and heat rose from the valley floor the way it does from a hot cast iron skillet. Falcons made lazy circles in the sky and grouse ran from one sage bush to another across the oxen's path.

Mary rode on the wagon seat beside Sam. Neither said much. After so many months on the trail there wasn't much to say that the other hadn't heard thousands of times before.

If they had made the trip two years earlier they would have passed three settlements along the river before getting this far. The founders of the small settlements chose to build close to the river, where trappers and traders could get in and out easily. They had no way of knowing about the massive walls of water that move down the rivers following years of heavy snowpack in the mountains. Two years before, a warm moist storm front passed over the mountains and the melting snow filled the streams to overflowing. The main stem of the Chinook River rose thirty feet over its normal banks. The settlements vanished with most of their inhabitants.

THE CHINOOK RIVER PRINCESS

On their third night in the Chinook Valley Sam and Mary set up camp under a large cottonwood tree close to the river. Sam collected sun-bleached sticks of cottonwood from along the riverbank and built a fire. It was luxurious to have a wood fire rather than the smoldering buffalo-dung fires they used on the prairie.

Sam, in his bare feet, cooked a simple meal of beans, bacon and unleavened biscuits. Mary sat on the protruding hub of the wagon's front wheel. By the dim light from the fire, she darned Sam's socks. Sam had only one pair of wool socks and they were now more cotton darning yarn than wool.

"Iz ready Miss Mary." Sam padded across the dirt in his bare feet and put a scoop of beans on each of the two tin plates balanced on one of the large fireplace rocks that Sam had pushed into place..

"I'm starving. It smells heavenly."

"It smells, Miss Mary, same as always."

"Here are your socks. We had better find some kind of trading post or store pretty soon or I'll have to start darning your feet instead of your socks."

"That might smart a mite." Sam handed Mary her plate.

"Thank you, Sam." Mary took her plate and went back to the wagon wheel. She sat on the hub again and balanced her plate on her thighs.

Sam sat cross-legged beside the fire, his tin plate on his lap.

"I'm sorry I brought you out here, Sam." Mary spoke quietly as she pushed some beans on her fork with a hard biscuit.

"Why's dat?"

"You seem so out of place out here. You're used to working with your back, loading and unloading things. Here you sit day after day on that damn wagon seat, losing all of your strength."

"I feels better'n I'ze ever felt afore, Miss Mary. I doan feels like I'ze missin' much bys not carrying bacca or pushing thems bacca casks."

"I'm glad to hear it. I was afraid you were miserable."

"No, Miss Mary. I'ze jus 'bout happy as ever was in ma life."

Sam was putting more wood on the fire and Mary was scrubbing their tin plates with handfuls of dirt when they heard a horse snort a short distance away. They both stopped what they were doing instantly and looked into the darkness beyond the firelight. The flickering flames sent rays of orange glow out into the darkness where it danced across the ground. Mary quit rubbing the tin plate she had been cleaning and stood up straight. Then she slowly moved closer to Sam.

In a few moments, Sam could just make out the image of a man on horseback. Slowly the image came closer, like a ghost approaching silently. The horse seemed to be walking on pillows, lifting its legs high and setting them down deliberately, easily.

Finally horse and rider were within the ring of firelight. It was an Indian straddling a spotted pony. He was a proud, but very young warrior of a small band that had broken ranks with the Shahaptian Tribe nine years before. The pony he rode was from a strong line that would be known as Appaloosa. The young warrior carried an obsidian pointed spear adorned with two brown and white mottled feathers. The Indian guided his mount

THE CHINOOK RIVER PRINCESS

to a position effectively blocking Sam's access to the wagon, to the rifle that lay under the wagon's worn oak seat. The young warrior then maneuvered his horse toward them, forcing Sam and Mary away from the wagon. He pointed his spear toward the crest of the hill. They understood. They were to walk in front of him.

A full moon lighted their way as they stumbled on jagged rocks and short scrub that shredded the hem of Mary's dress. It was lucky that Mary had finished darning Sam's socks and he was now wearing his heavy leather boots.

After traveling several hours, they arrived at a camp on a small tributary stream of the Chinook River. The camp was a temporary one the Indians used during the fall run of Salmon to stockpile smoked and dried fish for the winter months. As they moved toward the center of the camp where a large communal fire burned, three men approached them. They spoke a language of chopped syllables, resembling nothing they had heard before. After a brief animated exchange, Mary and Sam were separated.

Mary found herself confined in a hide-covered structure supported by wooden poles and warmed by a small ember-rich fire. There was an ancient looking woman who sat lifeless as a stone statue in the dim firelight, coming alive only to add small sticks to the flickering flames.

In a similar lodge, Sam paced the hard-packed earth like a caged cat. Unlike Mary, who accepted this new development as ordained by her newly rediscovered deity, Sam was seized with anxiety. He kept reproaching himself for not dealing with the red-skinned boy back at the wagon, when he had at least a small chance of success.

Mary lay upon a bed of pine boughs covered with several heavily-furred skins and claimed as deep and peaceful a sleep as any prisoner ever had. She was lulled by the quiet incantations of the old woman, who watched her as the smoke from the fire drifted up and out the small vent located at the highest point of the lodge.

Mary was awakened at sunrise by the abrupt entrance of a tribal elder. He stepped into the lodge, ducking under the skin door-flap that he pushed back with his right arm. He assumed a squatting position just inside the doorway and held the flap back to let the light of the early morning sun illuminate the prisoner. It was then that the old woman came to life. The ancient relic spoke in a gravelly voice that sounded as if it were coming from the bottom of a deep well. Mary felt a chill as the hair bristled on the back of her neck. The old warrior's jaw dropped in surprise at the old woman's words, then he turned and left as abruptly as he had come. When the door flap fell closed behind him, the interior of the lodge to returned to almost total darkness.

Within moments, another intruder burst into the lodge. It was a man, every bit as much of a relic as the old woman. His waist-length hair was thin from age and as white as a cloud on a cold winter day. He was draped in cougar skins and had several necklaces of teeth and bones. Leather pouches hung from his neck. As he stood motionless just inside the entrance, staring at Mary, the old woman spoke in her "bottom-of-the-well" voice. When she had finished, the white-haired relic slowly moved to where Mary sat upon her bed of hides. He

THE CHINOOK RIVER PRINCESS

stared for several moments at her right hand which lay beside her on the dark bison robe. Then he took her hand in both of his and lifted it gently, as if it were a wounded sparrow, and pressed it to his forehead. His eyes rolled up as if he were trying to see out of the vent in the roof without lifting his head. He spoke what seemed to be a chant of melodic gibberish as her father's ring rested upon his brow. After several moments the ancient shaman returned Mary's hand to where it had been. He then turned his back to Mary and the old woman and left so quickly it seemed that only a gust of wind had momentarily blown open the entrance flap.

Mary heard the voices of several men speaking in animated tones outside the lodge and after about ten minutes, she heard the approach of several horses. Just about the time the horses arrived two young braves entered the lodge and motioned for her to come outside with them. When she was first brought to the lodge she had been led by the arm and forced inside. Now the braves treated her with deference, indicating where she was to go by pointing. When she exited the lodge she had to shade her eyes from the bright morning sun, and was surprised to see Sam standing quietly with several spear points pressing into his lower back. They were surrounded by at least twenty men. There was the old man, several others not quite so old who seemed to direct the action, and a number of young warriors.

The tallest of the elders spoke in a loud and clear voice. He wasn't speaking only to those present, Mary sensed, but to all—to the trees that surrounded the campsite, the grass which grew in patches where sunlight penetrated the canopy of evergreens, the rocks that protruded from the pine needle-packed forest floor, and the cloud-dotted sky. When he had finished what reminded Mary of a speech at an important holiday celebration back home, several braves lifted Mary to the back of a medium-sized pony and others helped Sam onto a good-sized horse. Then the same young warrior that had brought them indicated they were to follow him out of camp. Mary thought it odd that they had been forced to walk to the camp at the point of a spear only to be later invited to leave the camp on horseback, behind an escort.

Before the sun had reached its zenith, the trio reached the point near the river where they had left the wagon. Luckily, the team of oxen had only wandered several hundred yards further up the trail. Mary was glad they had insisted on oxen. She was sure that mules would be miles away by now. The warrior took the pony and horse that Sam and Mary had ridden and retreated into the forest without saying a word.

Sam hitched up the team and he and Mary quickly climbed into the wagon seat. Sam picked up the reins. The oxen leaned against the traces and pulled the wagon from the river's edge and up to the valley's flood plain.

As they continued up-river the terrain at the river's edge changed from dry earth, covered with short dry grass, to forest and then back again. They were right at the edge of two competing environments. In some areas, the soil was deep enough to retain sufficient moisture to maintain a conifer forest, and in others areas the shallow soil was underlain by volcanic residue that rapidly transported the ground water back to the streams before it had a chance to nurture the roots of anything larger than small scrub. Sometimes when they passed through

THE CHINOOK RIVER PRINCESS

forested areas, they caught quick glimpses of the young warrior, who seemed to be following them at a distance.

When they had first entered the Chinook River valley after leaving the Snake River, they had started seeing signs of the fall fish that were making their arduous journey upstream. Earlier runs of Salmon that fought their way up the spring-flood swollen rivers and struggled up the shallow, diminished streams of summer, had spawned and died. Leaving rotting carcasses behind to nourish the earth. It was now time for the third and final run of the year.

As each day passed, they saw more fish. At first there were only a few fish fighting to get up small almost dry stream beds that emptied into the main Chinook River. The few fish turned into hundreds, then thousands of Salmon, which spawned and then died. Nature responded by sending everything that could walk, fly, or crawl to the water's edge to take advantage of the carnage.

Mary rode nervously on the wagon seat next to Sam, for the land was alive with carnivores. There were bears with their cubs, wolves, mountain lions, badgers, wolverines, skunks, eagles, hawks and whatever else one could imagine feeding at the water's edge. At times, the smell of rotting fish became so overwhelming that the two travelers would gag incessantly.

Even though Sam was only minimally literate, he was a master at deciphering the picture language of maps and the maps that Mary's prospective husband had sent were extraordinarily detailed and accurate. It was mid-October when the wagon finally reached the fork of the Little Chinook River, at which time Sam was convinced they would make it to the ranch. He had doubted they would finish the trip when they left the train, and had been convinced that they would be food for the vultures when they were captives of the Indians. It was because of the Indians that Sam now slept with, ate with, and did everything else with, his rifle. It had become as much a part of him as a third little finger.

At times, the trail was little more than a footpath along the edge of the Little Chinook. When they finally reached a stand of Cottonwood trees, about seven miles upstream from the fork in the river, the path widened to a rutted roadway. It was just as the map indicated. In the clump of Cottonwoods, stood a weathered, wooden structure that served as general store and home for the storekeeper's family. The store, located in the front half of the building, served the twenty-two ranches that were scattered throughout the area, ranches started by enterprising easterners who had purchased large sections of the enormous parcel of land which had been granted, years before, by the King of Spain, to the Spanish governor of the territory.

Two short-haired mongrels ran out to harass the apathetic oxen. Several minutes later a woman came out from behind the house to investigate the disturbance. It was apparent that she had been doing laundry.

"How do you do?" She was drying her hands on the apron which covered her yellow print dress. "Welcome!"

"Hello," Mary was surprised at the woman's accent, which was clearly not northern or southern.

"I'm Mary Harper, and this," she said, indicating her companion, "is Sam Grande."

"I'm Beth McGrath." The women reached up to give Mary a hand. "Let me help you. That seat is awfully high up in the air."

"Thank you, Ma'am," Mary gratefully accepted Beth's hand then stepped down to the top of the wagon wheel, and then to the hub, before jumping to the ground.

"Ma'am," the woman said in mock complaint. "Do I really look that old?"

"I'm sorry . . ." Mary hesitated a moment, "is that Mrs. McGrath?"

"Yes, my husband is Bret McGrath. We own this general store."

"Oh, a store . . . that's just what I need. We're in want of some supplies. I'm sick of dried beans." Mary whined, "I've eaten so many you could shell me and put me in a pot for dinner."

"No thank you." Beth wrinkled her nose. "I've had my fill of 'em too."

"Where are you heading?" Beth wondered what a white woman and a black driver were doing traveling alone in such country.

"Jus' up trail a piece," Sam interjected, "ta Mista March place."

"You mean John March's ranch?" Recognition came quickly to Beth's face. "Well I'll be," her voice raised almost to a squeal, "you're John's betrothed, aren't you?"

"Yes," Mary answered with a blush coming to her cheeks.

"Good gracious, girl. We've been waiting your arrival all summer. Now you come right in the house and have some biscuits and I'll put a tub of water on the stove for your bath."

"My bath?"

"Yes, Ma'am!" Beth placed her hands on her hips like a mother preparing to scold her kid. "You don't want to meet your new husband with two weeks of trail in your hair."

Chapter 13

Mary found it very easy to get used to being under a roof again. She hadn't sat in a kitchen chair in over a year-and-a-half, and she hadn't realized how comforting it was to sit inside a solid structure. The kitchen, with its stove and cupboards, made Mary feel at home. Beth put a large pan of water on the stove to heat for her bath, and as she watched her move around the kitchen, Mary wondered how old Beth was. She had firm muscles in her arms, and the skin on her arms and neck seemed tight, but her face was so dry and leathery from the effects of the weather that she looked older than women in Baltimore who were in their forties. Mary was also starting to show effects of the western climate, having been almost two years on the trail, but she still had a peaches and cream complexion by western standards.

"How long have you been out here?" Mary was trying to get an idea of Beth's age.

"Let's see," Beth stared out the kitchen window as if the answer were written on the side of the hill that rose from behind the house, "I came out three summers ago." She was recalling just how it had been before she had come.

"Both you and your husband . . .?" Mary hesitated, trying to remember his name.

"Bret," Beth said, relieving Mary's anxiety.

"Bret, Bret McGrath. Of course!" Mary remembered that Bret and Beth were the couple Father O'Brien told her about. "Father O'Brien told me about your coming out to marry Bret."

"That's right. He sent for me, just like John did you. I was eighteen and more than a little willin' to leave Connecticut. Bret had this store two years before he realized he needed a wife."

Mary could hardly believe it—if Beth had been eighteen when she left Connecticut and had spent two years on the trail, then three years here, she was only about twenty-three years old.

"Have any children?" Mary was sure that she must after having been married three years.

"Heavens no . . . thank the lord," Beth was obviously relieved or at least wanted Mary to believe she was. "I'm so busy now I don't know what I'd do if I had kids to worry about."

Sam sat on the porch and rocked himself to sleep in a big old chair that someone had built using two large barrel slats for the rockers, while Mary soaked in a hot tub in the kitchen. Beth had strung a line from the hat rack by the kitchen door to a frying-pan hanger on the adjacent wall, over which she had thrown a blanket to give Mary some privacy.

Mary slouched down in the tub, and at that moment was sure that heaven was a warm bath. As she sat in the steaming water, she soaked off about two pounds of grime that she had acquired and gained back a lot of femininity that she had lost along the trail. There's nothing quite so effective as a hot bath under a solid roof to remind a woman that she's a lady.

Beth was standing next to the stove where she and Mary could see each other as they chatted. Mary could see that Beth was a beauty, in spite of what the sun and dry air had done to her delicate skin. She had high cheekbones and a delicate nose and mouth that were framed by tawny, shoulder-length hair.

"What is Mr. March like?" Mary rubbed the bar of lye soap with the wash cloth.

"Mr. March?" Beth was incredulous. "Since when does a bride-to-be refer to her future husband as mister?"

"Since I don't know the man . . . that's since when," Mary couldn't hide her embarrassment.

"You'll get over that soon enough, I expect." Beth stared from the kitchen window at nothing in particular.

It was a pensive look that Mary saw in Beth's eyes. "Is he tall?" Mary's question brought Beth's thoughts back into the kitchen.

"Oh my, yes. He's just about as tall as they come, and good looking . . . in a harsh kind of way," she seemed to be visualizing him at that moment, "and he speaks in a deep but quiet voice."

"Well," Mary was pleased at what she heard, "he sounds like a perfect catch. Why did he have to send back east for a wife? It seems he'd have no trouble finding one."

"There aren't many unwed women in these parts, and John wanted a woman from the east, because . . . well, let's face it dear," she said placing her hands on her hips and cocking her head a little to the side, "any woman who grew up out here is heavy on the man and light on the woo, if you understand me."

"What was John's wife Anne like?" Mary used the question to try out the sound of her future husband's given name. "Was she pretty?"

"Heavens no!" Beth's look could only be described as disgusted. "That's just what I was saying—she was born out here. The land made her plain and hard. She was a worker, mind you, and would have made a good mother if she had lived long enough, but she wasn't much to look at. Bret told me that John always said that all the pretty ones came from back east, and that John was forever joking about sending back east to get a wife like Bret did . . . and wouldn't you know, he up and did it.

Mary flushed at the prospect of being considered a prize catch—until she met Jacob she hadn't thought of herself as being desirable. People were always saying what a pretty thing she was, and how she'd make some man very happy someday, but she had been sure they were just being kind.

They heard the buckboard pull up along side of the house.

"That'll be Bret," Beth walked toward the back door, "he was delivering a roll of wire to your new neighbor, Char Wilson."

Before Beth had a chance to stop him, Bret pushed open the kitchen door and burst into the room. Since the blanket that Beth put up for Mary's privacy was hanging between the tub and the front door, Mary had to slide down under the surface of the bath water to get out of his sight, and Beth started hitting her startled husband on his shoulders and back with the flats of her hands. "Don't come in here! Can't you see that a lady's bathing?"

"How's I supposed to know!" he complained as he headed back the way he'd come, looking over his shoulder, hoping to get another glimpse of the angelic form he had seen in the tub.

"Go into the store and make yourself useful until we're done in here."

"Okay, okay," He held his hands up and surrendered fully, "but how's I supposed to know you'd turned the kitchen into a bath house?"

"On second thought," Beth added, slapping Bred once more across the shoulders, "ride on over to John's place and tell him that his new bride is here, if he'd like to meet her . . . after she gets her trappings on."

When he'd gone, Beth noticed that Mary was still submerged. She shouted, "He's gone, you can come up now!" but being submerged, Mary couldn't understand her. Beth had to haul her up by the hair.

"I thought you'd drown," Beth was laughing, holding Mary up by the hair as she'd hold a possum by the tail..

"I liked to," Mary gasped after she caught her breath. "I've never been so embarrassed!"

"Oh, it's not that bad. Now you better dry yourself before Bret gets any ideas about marching through here again. I think he's going to be as randy as a goat after getting a glimpse of you . . . and you can bet that tonight I'll pay for it.

She'd never met any woman so outspoken as Beth before, and was more embarrassed by her comments than by Bret's glimpsing her bare shoulders.

"You'd better hurry. I sent Bret after John and I imagine that John won't be wastin' much time getting here."

"John?" Mary put her hands to her mouth and gasped, "Now?"

"Yes, now," Beth accentuated the word 'now.' "Aren't you the least bit anxious?"

"I'm scared to death. What if he doesn't like me?"

"Yes, I know, and what if cows walked on two legs? There isn't a man within two hundred miles that wouldn't just love to give you a roll."

Again Mary flushed as brightly as an autumn sunset. She was quickly learning to resent Beth's brashness.

Mary put on her best calico print that she pulled from the bottom of her steamer trunk. Even as wrinkled as it was, it was prettier than anything that could be purchased west of the Mississippi. She was afraid that her hair would still be a wet mess when John came, but the warm dry breeze made quick work of it.

She was standing primly on the porch next to Sam's chair, wringing her hands, when John and Bret finally came into view. She first glimpsed him as he came from behind a large Cottonwood. He appeared every bit as big as Beth had said. He reined in his horse so that it stopped beside the porch right beside where Mary stood, and Mary's breath came up short.

He wore a large-brimmed, chestnut-brown, beaver-felt hat. It cast a shadow across the upper part of his face. His profile was magnificent; he had a straight long nose, deep-set eyes, and was everything that she had ever fancied in a man. He was mounted on a painted horse, and he wore a full leather Argentine drape below the

THE CHINOOK RIVER PRINCESS

waist. The leather drape protected his legs from the thick brush that grew in the washes between the high hills.

In the past several months, she had wondered if any man could measure up to Jacob. At that moment she was sure that John could more than measure up, if he was anything close to being the man he looked.

"Miss Harper." He nodded and removed his hat which left a ridge in his thick brown hair. "I'm John March."

"Well, Mr. March," Mary almost choked on her words. "I'm so very pleased to meet you . . . and this is Sam Grande. He accompanied me on my journey."

"I am very pleased to meet the man who brought you across the country, " He nodded to Sam. "I'll be forever in your debt."

"Da debt be mo than paid, if in ya can jus hep me fine work in these parts, Mista March."

"You look like quite a strong man. If you can get a wagon across the flats and mountains you can find work most anywhere. I would appreciate having you work for me on my ranch. I have need of good hands."

"I stays long's ya needs me, Mista March."

"Call me John, Sam."

"Yessa, Mista John." Sam rose to his feet.

John smiled at Sam's reply, and at that moment Mary knew that all was going to be well—his smile was just like her father's.

Chapter 14

John drove the wagon. Mary sat on the seat next to him, while Sam rode along side on John's Paint. About two miles east of McGrath's store they passed within a hundred yards of the edge of a pine forest that extended down a wash from the higher hills. John scanned the tree line and noticed an Indian on horseback. He was in the shadows, just inside the tree line. He was sure the Indian wasn't trying to be secretive. He had learned from experience that the only Indian you see is one who wants to be seen.

"If you look very hard," he said, nodding his head almost imperceptibly toward the pines, "up there in the trees, you'll see an Indian."

"Oh, that's the one that took Sam and me to his camp and kept us overnight. He's been following and watching us ever since." She then told John of their harrowing experience with the Indians as he stared at her in disbelief. When she finished he drove in silence for a few hundred yards.

"They've been giving us fits for over a year." He cleared his throat. "They're fed up with all the ranchers coming into the area. They've taken to capturing lone wagons and scaring the devil out the drivers. They usually keep the drivers for several days at their camp. They scare them half to death, burn their wagons, and make them walk about fifty miles to the nearest ranch. It tends to discourage new-comers".

"Why didn't they do that to us?"

"I don't have any idea," he wrinkled his brow, "or why the hell he's watching us."

John drove the team in silence for a few moments more, then asked, "Weren't you scared?"

"I was scared half to death," Mary grabbed his arm and hugged it to her. Then she rested her head on his shoulder, "but the old Indian lady that watched over me made me feel safe. She sent for the white-headed old man and I think he convinced the others to let us go."

"White-headed old man?"

"There was this old man. He was draped in skins. He wore several necklaces of bones and teeth. He had white hair down to his waist. He came to see me. He acted really strangely."

"How do you mean?"

"Well, he . . . sort of sang. He closed his eyes like he was praying, and sang quietly. Then he put my right hand on his forehead."

"I can believe he thought you were an angel," he smiled warmly, "but it sounds like he thought you were some kind of god."

"How could he?"

"I don't know, but you're lucky he did. That's probably why that one's watching you." He nodded toward the brush at the edge of the woods. "The old man must have told him to watch you, to see what kind of magic you make."

Mary didn't put much stock in John's hypothesis, but held her tongue. She didn't have a better theory to offer, because, unlike the shaman she called the "Old Man", she had not glimpsed the future of mankind.

The old man, as Mary called him, had inherited the position of tribal storyteller, historian, and healer from his father. His father had inherited the position from his father, and he his, for as far back as the tribal memory reached. It was a history of thirty-seven generations, which he had committed to memory. Besides the tribal history, the old man had inherited the powers of the spirits. He learned to see into the spirit world. He had mastered all of the ritual medicines to heal the sick and allow earth-bound tribal members to see beyond their horizon-limited vision.

It was in his thirty-second summer, when he was still a young and untried shaman, that he first saw the red-eyed snake—a snake he wouldn't see until many years later on Mary's hand. He had traveled several weeks to the north, to the falls of the floating rock. He was in quest of a vision, seeking inspiration or guidance from the spirits, hoping that they would make known some secrets that could help him help his people.

He spent many days and nights on a small precipice overlooking the rock that floated on the water at the top of the falls in the valley of the yellow rocks. It was near the area where steam rose from the ground—the place the Indians called the valley of the gods' winter breath.

He made a circle of small stones about four feet across on a ledge beside the falls. He placed a water pouch made from a deer's stomach just outside of the circle.

He walked slowly and carefully into the circle and stood in the exact center. Then he crossed his legs at the

THE CHINOOK RIVER PRINCESS

ankles, bent his knees and very slowly sat down. He loosened the leather thongs that secured a small deerskin pouch around his neck. He emptied the contents of the pouch on the dirt before him. There were several special smooth stones, a skull from a mole, three bear teeth, a bear claw, and ten small dark seeds. He picked the seeds from the dirt one by one, then set them in a small pile beside his right knee. He then picked up each of the other items and put them back in the pouch, which he retied around his neck.

He picked up one of the small dark seeds between his thumb and forefinger and brought it to his mouth. He put it between his teeth and bit it open. It gave off a sweetly pungent odor that rose behind his palate to his nasal passages. He chewed the seed carefully, making sure to grind in into the finest mash with his teeth. He then reached out, grabbed the dear-stomach water bag and lifted it carefully in order not to disturb the circle of stones. He brought the bag up to his lips and drank. He drank slowly, letting the water slip down his throat almost too far before swallowing. He drank until the bag was empty.

He would not drink or eat anything but more seeds, until a vision or his death came. He ate one seed at sunrise each morning. It was about noon of the eighth day when the vision took over his consciousness.

As he shed his earthly shell, his mind turned inward, joining his spirit and those of his forefathers. The vision was like a dream, except so clear and real that he could reach out and touch the things that moved through it. You can't touch the things of dreams, only the things of visions.

In his vision were white doves and black ravens sitting in a leafless tree which did not touch the ground. The doves perched in the right half of the tree, the ravens in the left. There was a line of many men and women approaching the tree, one by one. The line of marchers was so long that it reached out of sight. Each marcher had a red-eyed snake intertwined in the fingers of one hand. When each marcher, in turn, reached the foot of the tree, the serpent he was carrying spoke of lives given, or taken. If a snake said it saw two lives taken, it would transform into two ravens on the marcher's hand and they would fly up and take their place next to the ravens in the tree. If a snake testified to so many lives given, it would turn into that many white doves and join the other doves in the tree.

It was nothing like the vision he was hoping for. Its meaning was so obscure that he would spend the next forty-one years searching for its significance. While he hadn't understood the full meaning of the vision, he recognized the importance of there being more doves than ravens when the last marcher in line finally reached the tree. He grew old waiting for the vision to have significance.

When, as an old man, he finally saw the red-eyed snake on Mary's right hand, the purpose of the vision was clear. He knew he had to prevent the white woman from taking any lives, which would make more ravens in his visionary tree. It was for that reason he sent his great-grandson to watch over her. The gods were asking for his help and the old man, through his son's grandson, would honor the sacred request.

As Mary had sat in the lodge with the old woman, the old man had briefed his great grandson, the young

THE CHINOOK RIVER PRINCESS

warrior. It was well that the young man had a deep respect for the wishes of his ancestors. He understood the importance of his great grandfather's vision to all of their tribe, past and present. He didn't understand, at the moment, that the mission to which his great-grandfather was committing him, would last a very long time.

The wagon bumped down the gradual rocky bank into the swiftly moving water. It was the widest and most shallow point in the river for twenty miles in either direction and the only place where a wagon could cross safely.

"Well, there it is." John nodded toward the other side of the river.

"There's what?" Mary could see nothing different from what she had seen for the last ten miles.

"The ranch." He said the word with surprise as if he had expected her to recognize it. He had been born and raised here and each rock and clump of grass was as familiar to him as Mary's front yard in Baltimore had been to her.

"I don't see a ranch." Mary looked for a fenced yard or something that set it apart from the rest of the terrain.

"It's all that you can see, from here to the top of the farthest hill straight ahead, and as far as you can see to the east."

"That must be five miles up the river and several to the mountain!"

"It's seven miles up river and about a mile-and-a-half over the hills."

"Where's the ranch or house or whatever you call the place you live?"

"The house is about a mile further up river, on a hill about a thousand feet above this point."

They followed the trail east along the south side of the Chinook River until it turned South into the out-wash of a stream that lay in the hollow between two massive hills. The hills were covered with long dry grass the color of ripe wheat.

"That's almost straight up!" She stared at the steep hillside.

"It's not so steep when you get used to it." John had no idea if his statement were true or not. He had been raised on these hills and didn't know that there was any flat land in the world until he was ten years old, when he went on his first cattle drive.

The double-rutted trail in the grass crossed the face of the hill from one switch-back to the other ten times, rising almost a hundred feet with each traverse of the hill face. When they finally reached the house, located in the flat area at the summit, Mary was overwhelmed with the view. She had to fight off a spell of dizziness that threatened to make her nauseous. The plains of the mid-west were expansive and the openness was a shock, but it was nothing compared to the expanse of God's earth that confronted her now. The hillside in front of her fell away so quickly, that she felt as if she were standing on the top of a ball. The slope continued to fall away below the part of the hill that she could see until it reversed slope near the bottom just before it met the river, which looked as if it were a string laying at her feet. She was afraid that she was going to fall, start rolling down the hillside, and not be able to stop until she reached the river.

THE CHINOOK RIVER PRINCESS

The opposite side of the river looked much like the side on which she was standing, and from where she stood she could see the river winding through the hills about ten miles to the west. It seemed as if she should be able to see the ocean from where she stood, even though she knew it was many hundreds of miles away.

"Oh my gosh, John, it's magnificent. This must be the world as God sees it!"

Chapter 15

The house was a large but simple mud-chinked log structure with a small porch perched at the top of six steps. Fifty yards southwest of the house were a barn and bunkhouse of similar construction.

John halted the wagon at the front steps then turned to Mary. "You'll sleep in the main house and I'll sleep with Sam and the hands in the bunkhouse until the wedding."

Sam climbed off the Paint.

"You can put the horse in the barn, Sam." John pointed beyond the house. "Just unsaddle her and tie her to one of the posts in the center. Then brush her down and put her in the second stall from the end. After you put her up, I'd like your help unloading the wagon."

"Yessir, Mr. Marsh."

John grabbed Mary by the waist and lowered her to the ground easily, as if she were made of feathers.

Mary smiled at John. "My, you're strong." She was surprised to see his face flush.

Mary climbed the well-worn steps to the front door. The steps were made of rough hewn logs but years of use had worn them shinny and smooth. John took off his hat as he pushed the door open in front of Mary. They stepped into the cool, dark house. It was hard for Mary to see until her eyes adjusted; when they finally did adjust, she could see it was a wonderful home. The floors were yellow pine and the ceiling was the yellow pine floor of

THE CHINOOK RIVER PRINCESS

the second floor nailed over the long lodge-pole pine stringers. The kitchen was straight back down the hall; on the table there were flowers in a vase sitting in a pool of sunlight from the kitchen window.

"I hope you like your new home." John stood stiffly, working the brim of his hat in his calloused hands.

"It's beautiful. I can see a woman's touch everywhere—the quilt on the wall, the nicknacks on the mantle, the punched-paper shade on the oil lamp."

"That was Anne; always adding something here or there to make it more homey."

"She did a great job. I hope I can live up to her example."

"Oh, I'm sure being from back East you'll know how to make it even more beautiful. Do you want to see the rest of the house?"

"I'd love to."

John lead the way down the hall to the kitchen. Mary followed slowly, looking at and noticing everything, the deep grain of the wood plank walls and the cobwebs where the ceiling and walls met.

"This is the sink," John proudly placed his hand on the handle of the water pump, "genuine porcelain over cast iron. I had Bret order it from Saint Louis and the pump, too. It pumps water from the cistern under the house. The tin roof catches all the rain and it goes into the cistern."

"Mighty ingenious." Mary nodded her head and smiled.

"There's the stove." John drew Mary's attention to it with his outstretched arm.

"It's a fine stove, John. I know because I used to sell them for Mr. Weed at his store in Baltimore."

"The boys and I built a firewood shed against the back wall here," he said, pointing to a door in the back wall. "You won't have to go outside for firewood. We keep the shed full of wood and you can just open the door and get wood whenever you want."

"That's wonderful. I bet Anne really appreciated it."

"She sure did. She loved the kitchen, she sewed the curtains. I wanted to buy some from Bret's and Beth's store but Anne said she didn't want any store-bought linens hanging at her windows."

"Ann must have been a wonderful wife."

John looked uneasy. "Yes, but she's gone and you're here now."

"She may be gone, John, but I don't want you to ever forget her. She'll always be a part of this household." She didn't know if she had said the right thing because John's eyes turned glassy.

"Let me show you the bedrooms upstairs," He walked quickly past Mary to stairway off the hall. She followed him up the narrow winding staircase, which opened into another hallway.

Mary stuck her head in the doorway in the middle of the hall and then brought it out and looked first down the hall to the left and then right. "Three bedrooms?"

"My grandfather built the house big because he wanted lots of children."

"Do you have many aunts and uncles?"

"None. My grandparents had four boys and a girl . . . all but my father died."

"How's that possible?"

"It's a hard land. Two of my father's brothers died from childhood disease and the other was killed when he was fifteen, when his horse stumbled and fell on the hill in front of the house. The horse rolled over him before tumbling half way to the river below. The girl died in the barn when she was six years old. She fell from the hayloft in the barn into a hay pile and landed on the tines of a pitchfork a young ranch hand had left in the hay."

"How tragic." Mary was suddenly worried that she might not be up to the trials of this harsh new land.

It was more harsh than she knew because what John didn't tell her was that his grandfather had run the young ranch hand through with the same pitchfork the young man had left in the hay. The whole valley knew how "Old Man" March had killed the hand in a rage but none faulted him for it. It was a hard and unforgiving land that made hard and unforgiving citizens.

"This will be your room." John walked to the front bedroom, "and our room after we're married."

"If there are three bedrooms, why will you sleep the bunkhouse with the men?"

"I can't sleep under the same roof with you until we're married."

"But why not?"

"My father always said that a man and woman couldn't sleep under the same roof until they were married."

"I think he. . ." Mary stopped, realizing that she couldn't explain what John's father really meant without making John feel a bit foolish. Her future husband would be no one's fool, especially not hers.

"You think he what?"

"I think he was a fine man with a fine set of values."

"None finer," John smiled proudly.

Mary noticed the quilt on the bed. It was covered with rambling rose vines and many red roses on a background of pink.

"Don't tell me. . . Anne made the quilt."

"Yep. She was a wonder."

"It's too beautiful to be laying on the bed in the sunshine; it'll fade. We'll have to hang it on the end wall, away from the light." She was thinking that she could live with everything else in the house that was Anne's, but she'd be damned if she and her new husband would make love under a quilt made by the loving hands of his previous wife.

John took Sam into the bunkhouse. It was a low, one-story structure with a row of six beds against the long wall and a pot-bellied stove at the far end.

"The first three beds on the left are taken. I'll be using the one at the end beside the stove. You can have either of the two that are left."

"I thinks I be taken da one on da left." Sam was unsure how Mr. March would take to having him in the next bed.

John was pensive for a moment. "On second thought, I think you should take the one closest to mine. I'm not at all sure that the boys will appreciate having a new neighbor."

Sam thought, you means a new nigger neighbor, doesn't ya? Sam walked over and put his bag at the foot of the bed beside Mr. March's.

THE CHINOOK RIVER PRINCESS

John was back in the main house and Sam was lying on his bunk when Clarence, Brody, and Walt came in from their long day. They eyed Sam with curiosity.

"You're one big nigger," Brody, the tall skinny one said.

Sam got up from the bunk. "Ize Sam."

The short chubby one with shaggy hair spoke up, "I'm Clarence and this here's Walt. The one with the sharp tongue is Brody."

"Honored," Sam replied, trying to be as friendly as possible, not wanting to cause any trouble in Mary's new home.

Brody shot back, "Well I ain't honored. Since when did Marches start hiring niggers? There wasn't no cotton on this ranch last time I looked."

Sam was silent.

"I'm speaking to you black boy."

Clarence spoke up. "Leave him alone, Brody. Mr. March must have put him in here."

Brody cut him off by raising his hand as a signal for silence. "And who's bunk is that?" Brody pointed to the one on the end. "Is that another nigger's bed?"

"Clarence is right, Brody. Leave him alone," Walt said.

"That's right," a voice said from the doorway.

All the faces turned to see John coming in the door.

"I didn't hire on to bunk with no nigger, Mr. March."

"Well that's fine, Brody, because we don't have any here. All we have here is my new hand Sam Grande."

Brody's neck grew in anger. "I don't see any new hand named Sam. All I see is one big nigger."

John stepped close to Brody and backhanded him smartly on the right side of his face.

"I said that this is my new hand, Sam. He's taking your job."

"My job?"

"Your job. Now get your things together. You have five minutes to be on your horse and headed down to the main road."

Brody stared in disbelief.

"I said five minutes, Brody, now move."

Mary and John were married the following Sunday at the McGrath general store, with Beth, Bret, Sam and neighboring ranchers looking on. Mary wore the beautiful white high-bodice dress she had carried over two thousand miles just for the occasion and John wore a too-tight dark wool suit he received for his eighteenth birthday. When he was eighteen, the suit hung on him like window drapes. He also wore a narrow black bow tie that Bret loaned him.

At first Mary felt guilty wearing white but overcame her reservations with the thought that John had stood before the minister before with another woman. She wondered how much he had loved her and if he didn't still.

The wedding was in McGrath's store because it was the biggest room within fifty miles. All the merchandise had been pushed against the walls to clear the center of the room. There were twenty-six witnesses to the wedding and that included the elders of all the families of all the ranches withing thirty or so miles.

THE CHINOOK RIVER PRINCESS

Beth was fidgety before the ceremony. She bit her nails almost to the quick before the pair were pronounced man and wife. After the affair Beth was the only one who didn't congratulate the couple. Only Sam noted the omission. He was an empathetic soul and picked up on the slightest undercurrent.

After the couple had finished their vows, everyone retired to the large grass clearing behind Beth and Bret's store and house. Lewis Thompson had donated several pigs and William Bonner had donated a steer to the feast. The meaty carcasses had been roasting over fire pits since early morning and the meat was almost falling off the bones.

Ten tables from the store had been set up out back and three were covered with everything anyone could imagine. The variety of foods amply demonstrated that valley had ranchers from every European lineage. There were sausages, kraut, dumplings, stews, salads, fruits and all kinds of food that Mary had never seen or tasted before. It was all fabulous and, being the honored couple, Mary and John had to eat a little of everything.

That evening was so special it caught Mary by surprise. It's unbelievable what a simple ceremony can mean. When she said that she would take John for better or for worse until death would make them part, she felt a new bond and yet a freedom she had never known before. She felt everything was right with her, John, and the world for the first time.

Mary and John sat on their porch and watched the sky turn to fire in front of them; it turned into shades of blazing reds and orange by the sun setting below the ridge of the mountains behind them. The sky was almost as colorful every evening but the simple act of making a life-long commitment gives a beautiful sunset meaning that it never had before. Mary found that such commitment gives everything a meaning it never had before. The world was no longer an uncontrollable wild and scary place but a warm, tame and friendly place. She hugged John's bicep to her chest as they sat on the long bench. Whenever she looked up at John's stoic face she kept thinking: I'm married, and this is my husband.

When the last light of day had faded, the stars grew so bright it looked as if someone had thrown a popper full of popcorn on a black quilt. They sat perfectly still until the moon came up over the mountain in front of them, it's brightness dimming the light of the stars.

John had wondered about the snake ring on Mary's right hand and finally worked up the courage to speak of it. "That's an interesting ring you wear. Where did you get it?"

"Oh, yes, the snake. It was my father's. It was given to him by a man he saved from the sea. It was with his things the captain of his ship brought home after he was killed at sea."

"I'm sorry, I shouldn't have asked."

"It's all right, John. There isn't anything you shouldn't ask me."

"I think I'll be getting to bed now." He got up from the bench. "Tomorrow morning will come mighty early after such a busy day."

"You're right," Mary said, "Let's."

THE CHINOOK RIVER PRINCESS

When Mary slid into bed beside John, she was surprised how natural it felt. She gently rubbed his chest and he turned to her. He pulled her close and she straddled his leg; they kissed and she was consumed. She found it totally different from what had been between her and Jacob. What she and Jacob had was confined to the secrecy of the grasslands not blessed and not right in God's eyes and that did make a difference. In their own bed, blessed by God at a ceremony witnessed by the world, Mary's and John's union was totally righteous and uninhibited.

They kept waking throughout the night and making love as if it were for the first time. They weren't counting but if they had they would have reached a number less than eight, but more than six.

Chapter 16

The following morning, Clarence cooked the married couple a breakfast of sourdough biscuits, eggs, toast, a hash of potatoes and smoked beef, and sassafras tea. Mary had never felt so special.

"I feel like a princess," Mary said.

"You are a princess, the Chinook River Princess," John said seriously. "How would you like to see your kingdom?"

"What do you mean?"

"Tour the entire ranch."

"I'd love it."

"We'll saddle a couple of horses. Clarence can pack us a lunch, maybe even a supper since it's a mighty big ranch, and we'll spend the day exploring."

Mary was silent a long moment. "I don't know how to ride a horse."

John looked shocked. "Don't know how to ride? Didn't you just come across the entire country?"

"Yes, but in a wagon, not on horseback."

"I've never known anyone who didn't ride. It's something I'd never give a second thought."

"Well give it one. Is it hard to learn?"

"I don't really know. I don't remember when I didn't ride."

"I'm ready to learn."

THE CHINOOK RIVER PRINCESS

"We don't have a choice in the matter. You can't live on a ranch without riding a horse; a buggy just can't get us wherever we need to go."

"I said I'd learn, John. Right after breakfast you can teach me."

"All Right, Princess, right after breakfast and then we'll explore your new kingdom."

John would saddle the horses himself, showing Mary how it was done. He opened the gate of the first stall near the door, where the light was coming in the doorway and they could see better. He lifted a bridle off the peg on the gate post and walked into the stall.

"You have to move easily and smoothly to keep the horses from getting nervous, Princess. If you're nervous they'll sense it and wonder just what kind of no good you're up to."

"I know about horses. I said I have never ridden a horse before, not that I had never seen or been around horses before."

"I'm sorry, Princess. I'm just not sure how much you do or don't know."

"I won't say any more. Just tell me everything and if it's something I already know I'll just listen anyway."

"This is the bridle and this iron piece, called the bit, has to go in the horse's mouth. You just hold the bridle by this nose strap with your right hand, the head strap with your left hand, and slip it over the nose so the bit goes in the mouth, then pull the head strap over ears to rest on the back of the head. The ears will stick up between these two straps on the head. Then you buckle these two straps under the jaw and around the mouth."

"You make it look easy."

"It is rather easy. The hard part comes next." John pulled a saddle blanket off the top rail between the stalls and placed it gently onto the horse's back.

"Place the blanket on the horse's withers gently so you don't spook him."

"That doesn't seem so hard."

"What do you mean?"

"The hard part you said comes next." Mary had a mischievously smile on her lips.

"No, not the blanket, Princess, the saddle."

"Oh." She grinned.

John went out of the stall and picked up the saddle that was resting on the saddle tree made to hold the saddle while it aired out. He carried it back into the stall and with one easy sweeping motion, placed the saddle over the horse's withers.

"Next, you have to get the girth—the strap that goes under the stomach—really tight," he said, reaching under the horse's belly, retrieving the girth and then putting it in through the buckle on the near strap, then attaching another buckle to a further strap, "or the saddle will slide around the side of the horse and you'll wind up riding in what we call the under-belly position."

John pulled firmly but gently on the girth and it tightened around the horse's belly. "Give the horse a chance to exhale, so her belly will be smallest then pull the girth with all your might. Then check it to make sure it's really tight."

"It doesn't seem too complicated but I'm not sure I can lift a saddle high enough to get it on her back."

THE CHINOOK RIVER PRINCESS

"You won't be able to for a while but if you keep working at it, you will develop the strength to do it."

"I'm glad you have so much faith in me. Frankly, I don't."

"Princess, you can do anything you put your mind to."

"And how do you know that?"

"Sam told me."

John saddled another, then led the two horses outside. "You have to mount a horse on his left side."

"Why is that?"

"It's just a rule of convenience. Horses like things to stay the same and they don't like surprises. If everyone mounted their horse on whichever side they wanted, no one could ever be sure how to mount another's horse without spooking it. This way everyone knows if they spook a horse at least it wasn't because of trying to mount from the side the horse isn't used to."

"Are there many other rules I have to learn?"

"Thousands. You don't spit into the wind, you don't drink out of a stream before you look to see that a steer isn't making water in it..."

"That's enough, John. I don't want to know all of them right now. Just give me each rule as I need it."

"Fair enough, Princess. Now come over here so I can boost you up. Loop the reins over the horn, stand on your right leg, put your left foot in the stirrup here, grab the saddle horn with your right hand and swing yourself up and into the saddle at the same time."

John, not realizing how light Mary was, boosted her almost over the saddle and she had to work to get back to center.

"I'm sorry, Princess, I didn't realize you were as light as a pillow."

"You say the sweetest things, John."

"What do you mean?"

"Never mind. Just know that I love you."

John blushed and he stood perfectly still for a moment, then he turned and quickly mounted his horse.

"The first thing to learn is how to stop. You have to let the horse know who's boss and pull back on the reins hard if she doesn't want to stop."

"What if she won't stop?"

"Pull harder. That bit in her mouth will irritate her if you pull hard enough and she's not going to keep going if she doesn't like the way it feels."

"How do I make her go where I want her to go?"

"You just lay the reins over to the side like this," He demonstrated, "give a gentle push with your legs and she will go the way of the reins."

"That seems easy enough."

"It all easy. The hard part is convincing the horse that you're in charge. Once she realizes that, she'll do what ever you want her to."

"How do I convince her? Can't I just ask her nicely?"

"Only if you speak Spanish. Your horse came from Mexico and doesn't understand a word of English. Until you teach her English, you'll just have to kick her in the sides to make her go and pull back hard on the reins to make her stop."

"How long does it take to teach a horse English?"

"I was only kidding, Princess," John smiled and shook his head.

"So was I."

THE CHINOOK RIVER PRINCESS

John maneuvered his horse close to Mary's. "When you want to go, just say 'giddiyup' and dig your heals gently in her sides."

"Like this?" Mary did exactly what John told her.

"Just like that."

"Then why is she just standing here?"

"She thinks she's in charge. You'll have to be more firm. Say it louder and dig your heels in harder."

Mary dug her heels in the horse's ribs but the horse just turned her head and glanced at her as if to say, "Are you still here?"

Mary yelled "giddiyup" and buried both heels in the horse's ribs, convincing her horse it was time to go. The horse started at a gallop and John had to spur his horse to catch up.

"Now that I got her going, are you sure I can stop her?"

"There's only one way to know," John shouted after her, "pull up on the reins and say 'whoa.'"

Mary pulled back on the reins and said the magic word but her horse just kept galloping as if to say, "You wanted it so much, now you got it."

"Whoooooa!" Mary pulled the reins back until her horse's chin pulled back onto her neck. She then pulled back harder, until her horse abruptly stopped. Then the horse reared up and Mary instinctively leaned forward to keep her balance. She slid off the horse's back and landed on her feet for a moment before falling back on her bottom. Her full dress came up and exposed her legs up to her bloomers, she wasn't wearing petticoats.

"Are you all right, Princess?"

"I'm all right," Mary scrambled to her feet as she pushed her dress down, "but if this horse tries that again, I'll shoot her between the eyes!" Then the walked up to the horse's head and spoke into the horse's ear loudly, "Did you hear me? I'm going to shoot you between the eyes if you ever do that again."

Mary took the reins in her left hand, grabbed the saddle horn in her right hand, put her left foot in the stirrup and pulled herself up in one awkward motion. John sat, staring in disbelief. He had never met a more determined and formidable woman.

"Now let's giddiyap, you old hag!" Mary dug her heals in her horse's sides. Her horse started walking at a nice even pace.

"You're going to be one fine horsewoman, Princess."

"Thank you, John. You know you were wrong."

"About what?"

"This horse does understand English. She just likes playing stupid in front of men."

John spurred his horse to an easy lope and Mary's horse followed his lead. They crossed a wide expanse of grass on a hillside and then came to a finger of woods with a stream running through it. John reined his horse to a stop beside the stream and Mary did the same.

John stood up in his stirrups a moment, looked around, then relaxed. "Your horse seems to have learned her lessons well."

"Yes, hasn't she."

John pointed to a small rock structure in the stream and said, "This is Whiskey Creek and that's a dam my father built."

"What's it for?"

"It backs the water up to go into that ditch going out the other side of the woods."

"What for?"

"Out here, water is the difference between ranchers who make it and ranchers who fail. My grandfather and father spent their entire lives making this ranch into the best producing ranch in the whole Chinook Valley. They built dams like this and ditches like that all over this ranch to carry water to the crops. The ditches follow the hillsides for miles to bring water to the orchards and the wheat, barley, and corn fields."

"I didn't know you had orchards, or raised corn or wheat. I thought you were a cattle rancher."

"Cattle are fine when the winters aren't too harsh or the summers not too dry, but a bad season can kill most of a herd. A rancher can go broke paying his hands without a herd to sell."

"What kind of orchards do you have?"

"We, Princess, have fruit orchards. We have apples mostly, but some pears."

"Who do you sell the fruit to?"

"We cook and seal it in those new fangled tins in our cook house several miles up river and then haul the tins to Boise by wagon. We get fifteen cents a can in Boise."

"Fifteen cents?"

"Out here, fruit that can be eaten year round is a luxury people will pay for."

"What do you do with the corn?"

"We put some of that in tins also, for Boise, but most of it we let dry in the fields and then cut it and put the stalks in sheds for the cattle just in case we get a hard winter."

"You raise enough for all the cattle?"

"We have enough to keep the herd from starving to death. The cattle are mighty thin after a hard winter even with the corn, but they fatten over the summer. The other ranchers lose their herds every ten years or so. That's why this ranch is so big. Whenever a neighbor couldn't make it with his land payments and all, my grandfather and father would buy them out. We have over ten thousand acres now."

"That seem a bit heartless to profit from your neighbor's bad fortune."

"Dad and Grandad paid well for the land, they didn't steal it. They were always willing to show the other ranchers how to irrigate and raise crops to tide them over the hard times; too many of the other ranchers didn't listen. The only one who listened to my grandfather was Mr. Samuels, about ten miles down river. His grandchildren now have a four-thousand acre ranch."

"Why do you call this Whiskey Creek?"

"In my Grandfather's time, this was part of Old Man Walker's ranch. He was a steady drinker and used to go fifty miles downriver to buy his whiskey by the case. One day when he was coming home, he was going too fast when he crossed the creek and the wagon hit a rock. The case of whiskey hopped off the back and smashed down in the creek. From then on it was Whiskey Creek."

"It's an unusual way for a creek to get named isn't it?"

"Oh, no. They're all named after something that happened there or nearby. We have Squaw Creek, Papoose Creek, a bunch of Rattlesnake Creeks, Bear Creek, Elk Creek, Wolf Creek, Beaver Creek, and many others, including Naked Woman Creek."

"Don't tell me, let me guess."
"Yep, someone saw Grandma bathing in that one."

Chapter 17

The following months were a broadening experience for Mary. She learned to accept her new environment as easily as John's lovemaking. The gold band on her left hand gave her a sense of security that she hadn't felt since her father died. With each passing day her house perched in the golden hills became more like the home that had been torn from her.

Mary developed a love for the land that would have made John's grandfather proud. She seemed to come alive in the mountainous terrain. During the fall she worked her fingers to the bone clearing the irrigation ditches whenever she wasn't cooking or cleaning. Clarence was paid to be the cook as well as a ranch hand but Mary gave him much help. She got a certain satisfaction from preparing John's meals, just as her mother had for her father.

That first winter in her new home came early and it was a hard one. The first snow dusted the hills before Thanksgiving and by December the temperature never rose above freezing. The cattle herds moved carefully across the face of the hills. They pushed the shallow snow aside so they could eat the underlying dry grass. Just as the grass was stored beneath the snow for the wintering cattle, human forage was preserved in the ranch's cellars. The cellars were full of apples and potatoes as well as dried corn and hundreds of sealed

THE CHINOOK RIVER PRINCESS

glass jars and tins of vegetables and fruit. The woodpile held almost twenty cords of pine and, like the northern geese, all of the hands save Sam and Clarence had gone south for the winter.

That first winter served to bond the newlyweds. They became like frisky colts in each other's presence and the harsh weather outside accentuated the loving warmth that filled the cozy house. John was a very considerate lover and Mary found it not too difficult to put her experience with Jacob behind her.

One evening in early February John came in from the bitter cold after checking on the herds in the far eastern pastures to find Mary rocking quietly beside the warm stove with wet eyes.

"What's wrong, Princess? Why are you crying?"

"I don't know . . . sometimes women just cry."

"Come on, Princess," He took her face in his hands. "Tell me. Maybe I can make it better."

"You can't make it any better than it is—you'll never know how happy I am."

"Happy?" John raised his eyebrows. "Sitting here crying?"

"Oh, John. I am happy. So very happy . . . that's why I'm crying. I can't believe how happy you've made me," she said, looking into his deep-set brown eyes. "We're going to have a baby."

"A baby?" he mumbled, then shouted, "A baby?"

"Yes." Her eyes were aglow.

"A baby!" He turned and walked a few steps away before turning again and coming back to face her. "You're sure? A baby?"

"Yes I'm sure," she said, nodding.

He dropped to his knees, took her face in his hands again, and kissed her. "I'm so happy." He spoke as much to himself as to her. "A baby." He repeated the statement as if saying it would make him understand it better. He wasn't sure how he was supposed to feel. He thought that some special feeling was supposed to come over him but he wasn't feeling anything but a very deep closeness to Mary, and that wasn't a new feeling.

He pictured himself looking at Mary as she would rock her new baby. A warm feeling washed over him like sunshine on a summer afternoon. After several moments he got to his feet and shouted at the top of his lungs. "A baby! I'm going to be a father!" Then he ran out of the door, leaving it ajar, so that Mary had to get up and close it against the cold wind. John ran to the bunkhouse in just his shirt sleeves to tell Sam and Clarence. He felt that he would burst if he didn't tell someone. The snow was only a few inches deep on the ground and the blowing flakes almost filled John's footprints before she got the door closed behind him.

When he finally returned after sharing a pint of brandy with the only male companionship within five miles, he got his pipe from its resting place on the mantle, filled it, and pulled a chair up beside Mary's so he could hold her hand.

They sat hand in hand. They sat in silence that way for almost an hour. Then Mary got up and went into the bedroom.

"Are you going to bed now?" John wondered how he was supposed to treat a woman who was going to have a baby—his baby.

"No, I'm just going to get something."

THE CHINOOK RIVER PRINCESS

"Do you need any help? You're not supposed to lift anything heavy are you?"

"It's all right to lift things, John, but I'm not going to lift anything. Don't worry."

She opened her trunk that rested in the corner of the room and took out a small box that she carried back to the kitchen area as carefully as a child would carry a puppy. She sat down in the rocker again with the box in her lap. Then she told John about the fish she caught as a girl when she and Sam had lived in Baltimore, and about her last visit to her father's ship. When she finished, she handed the box to John.

"I want you to have this. I know he would want you to have it also. He would have liked you so very much." Tears welled up in her eyes.

John took the box, treating it as carefully as she had, and opened it slowly. When he looked inside tears welled up in his eyes also.

"It is the most gorgeous thing I've ever seen." He lifted the flame-grained pipe up high so that the light from the oil lamp illuminated the magnificent grain in the briar. "This is the finest gift anyone could ever receive. I know how much it means to you."

Mary took his left hand and put it to her lips, kissing it gently before putting it to her cheek. "I love you more than you could ever know, John."

"I think I do know." John pursed his lips in an effort not to show too much emotion.

In the spring, as soon as the snow melted, Mary started working on the irrigation ditches again. Then she put some of the ranch hands to work tilling the fields as soon as they returned from their winter migration.

Whenever she was working in the most remote parts of the ranch, she would occasionally get a glimpse of the young warrior. One especially pretty day she rode to the eastern-most boundary of the ranch to clear some rocks from the ditch near the diversion on Rocky Creek. She dismounted the beautiful sorrel mare that John had given her for her twentieth birthday. She stood quietly beside the big horse and glanced across the expansive valley. There was a herd of about twenty elk, or *wapiti* as the Indians called them, grazing on the opposing slope just below the edge of the forest. It was a magnificent sight and it inspired Mary to take a deep breath. She filled her lungs with the rich air.

The hills were covered with freshly sprouted grass, a blanket of translucent emerald. The stark contrast between this new green and the recently passed winter whiteness was a very welcome relief.

She was about seventy yards from the trees that marked the edge of the riparian habitat along the creek. She bent at the waist and started picking and tossing the smaller rocks from the muddy ditch, unaware that she was standing in the intended path of a grizzly bear and her cub. Her horse started to fidget as soon as it smelled the bears, but Mary was oblivious to the danger until the angry sow let out a bellow as it charged from the cover of the creek bed.

Being about seventy yards from where the bear began its attack, Mary could have outrun the old sow on her mare, if it hadn't bolted. It had, however, and she was left standing in the open as the seven hundred pound beast accelerated toward her. She had no time to contemplate the hopelessness of the situation. She turned and started running as fast as her legs would carry her. Luckily her pregnancy wasn't so far along that she couldn't run. She tripped and fell several times on the rocky, uneven ground but each time she regained her feet in an instant. She darted across the slope like a pronghorn antelope. She was so pumped-up with adrenalin that her hair stood straight out on the back of her neck and she didn't feel any pain from the abrasions on her hands and forearms. She refused to turn and look, knowing that impending death was right behind her. She hoped that when it caught her, it would finish her quickly.

It was after she had run about thirty yards and the bear had closed to within about twenty yards of her that she heard galloping hooves. She looked over her shoulder as she ran. To her amazement, the young warrior on his horse was coming fast behind the raging beast. He held his lance in his right hand with the shaft resting in the bend of his arm at the elbow, the pointed tip aimed at the back of the bear. He sighted along the shaft.

At a full run the horse passed within two feet of the bear as the spear's point penetrated the back of the hulk's neck just below the head. The spear's point slammed up through the base of the bear's brain, then smashed into the opposite side of the grizzly's two-inch-thick skull so hard that the spear splintered. The horse continued on and as it passed the bear, the ragged end of the broken shaft sticking from the bear's neck penetrated the lean skin covering the young warrior's chest. The ragged shaft skittered across his ribs, tearing a gaping hole in his flesh.

It was fortunate that the massive grizzly died instantly because the young warrior was incapacitated. The impact of the broken shaft upon his ribs and his head upon the ground had knocked him unconscious.

Mary fell to her knees and sobbed in relief. She rocked back and forth on her haunches for several minutes before she regained her composure. She got to her feet weakly and stood still for a few seconds. Her head was spinning and she was afraid she would faint. She walked slowly back to where the young Indian lay, the grass red with his blood. At first she thought he was dead, but then his ribs heaved as his body involuntarily drew breath.

Mary knelt beside the young warrior. Then she stood, grabbed his right arm, and pulled him over onto his back. She gasped when she saw the gaping wound in his upper side. She pulled up her skirt and then pulled down her cotton petticoat. She tore the petticoat into five-foot strips and wrapped the Indian's chest to stem the bleeding. He was a small man, weighing slightly more that she, and with much effort, she was able to wrestle him to the back of his horse. As she struggled with the warrior's limp body, she thought how angry John would be to see her attempting such a thing in her delicate condition. She finally got the young warrior positioned across the horse's neck. She grabbed the horse's mane and slowly led him back to the ranch house.

Chapter 18

Mary pulled the Indian from his horse and he fell to the ground hard in spite of her efforts to let him down gently. She gabbed him under the shoulders and dragged him up the front steps and across the porch. She rested a moment before she pushed open the door with her bottom and pulled the wounded man into her home. The dirt and dust from his loin cloth and the backs of his legs, and the blood from his bloody bandages left a trail. She had washed the floor just the day before, but it now looked as if someone had dragged a freshly butchered side of beef across the yellow-pine flooring.

She stoked the stove with a few pieces of dry rotten wood and blew on embers left from the breakfast fire. The wood smoldered and then burst into flames. Mary added pieces of wood of ever increasing size until the stove box was roaring with flames. She put her largest tin kettle on the stove top and filled it from the water bucket beside the back door. As the water heated, she rocked in her rocking chair and planned how she would clean the mess that lay on the floor at her feet. She had never nursed a wounded man before, but she knew she could do it well if she just approached the job like any other job, taking it one step at a time.

When the water on the stove began to boil, she poured a portion back into the wood-stave water bucket. She tested the temperature with her elbow, then poured in some more hot water and tested it again. She did the testing and pouring until she had it just right, or rather, until she didn't feel right putting off the job any longer.

She retrieved a strip of clean cotton cloth and a pair of scissors from her sewing basket. She carefully cut the bloody bandages from the warrior's back and then dipped the strip of cloth in the bucket. Then she squeezed out the excess water and opened the cloth. She started at the back of his neck and gently but firmly washed the Indian's lean body. When his back was completely clean and dry, she could postpone cleaning his wound no longer.

She lifted his left arm and placed it alongside his head. Then she grabbed his right arm and pulled him over onto his back. She winced at the sight of the ugly hole in the young man's side. The light from the window was insufficient, so she lit the oil lamp on the mantle and placed it on the floor beside him. The wound was ugly and dirty, but the edges of tear had stopped bleeding freely and were now only seeping a pinkish watery fluid.

She could see the white of his ribs through the parted flesh and muscle; the sight made her ill. She got to her feet in a rush and staggered to the back door. She leaned against the door frame and retched until her sides ached. About a minute after she finished retching she came back to his side. She dabbed the wound with the wet cloth, rinsing it often. She kept wiping the wound and flushing it with water until it was a fresh pink color and no longer dark with dirt.

She sat on her haunches for about ten minutes, staring at the gaping wound. Then she went to the kitchen cupboard and got the tin of sulfur. She sprinkled the sulfur liberally into and around the wound. She sat on her

THE CHINOOK RIVER PRINCESS

haunches again. She knew what had to be done, but she kept putting it off. Finally, she got to her feet and went to her sewing basket again.

She took the biggest needle from the pin cushion and a two-foot length of black bees-waxed carpet thread. She went to the front door where the light was good to thread the needle. Then she went back to the prone form on her floor. She tried to push the needle through the young man's hide at the edge of the wound but her fingers were damp and the needle just slipped between her fingers.

She went back to her sewing basket and got her prized silver thimble, the one Mrs. O gave her on her sixteenth birthday. As she pushed the needle through the man's skin with the thimble, Mary said, "No Mrs. O, this isn't the quilt you always pestered me to get started on. No, Mrs. O, I'm not particularly fond of sewing. Yes, Mrs. O, I would rather be fishing down at the pier. Yessiree, Mrs. O, I sure would rather be fishing." Then she grasped the needle hard between her left thumb and forefinger and pulled it the rest of the way through the young warrior's skin. As she stitched the edges of the gaping wound together, she noticed the ring on her finger felt warm, almost hot. She tired to slip it off but it wouldn't slide over her knuckle, even though her fingers were wet with blood. My fingers must be swollen, she thought.

As the Indian slept, Mary scrubbed the floor. She worked to get up the mud and blood streaks that showed where his body had been dragged across the floor. It was an easy floor to wash. There were fairly wide spaces between the yellow-pine planks, and as she scrubbed the floor with a soaking brush, the excess water drained right on through, dripping six inches to the dirt below. There was no basement like the homes had back in Baltimore because the dirt was only several feet deep over solid bed rock. It would take a ton of blasting powder to excavate a basement in the hills along the Chinook River. It must have taken a bunch of powder to blast out the cistern, she thought.

It was about sunset when John finally came in from the north pasture. She heard the rapid hoofbeat of his horse just before John reined him to a stop at the hitching rail. Then she heard his boots hitting the front steps in quick succession and knew he was running. The front door flew open and John stood in the open doorway, back lighted by the crimson sky. She saw the pistol in his right hand.

"Mary! Where are you?"

"I'm here, John," She spoke in a calm voice, "beside the stove."

John lowered his revolver. "What's the Indian's horse doing out here?"

"He's in here. He's hurt."

John gently placed the gun back into his holster as he walked slowly into the room. He was trying to make out the details of the things in the room in the dim light.

"I don't care if he is hurt. He shouldn't be in the house."

Mary quickly stood. "I was being chased by a grizzly bear and he killed it. He's staying right here until he's well."

John moved closer to the fireplace. In the dim light of the oil lamp he could see the Indian on the floor between the bunk, which Mary had drug from the bunkhouse, and the hearth. He was laying flat on his back, wrapped in a blanket like a caterpillar in its cocoon. His head was resting on a doughnut-shaped ring that Mary had fashioned from a pair of John's long Johns. She didn't want the nasty, bloody knot on the back of his head to rest on the hard floor. His long black hair was spread around his head like the splatter of black paint dropped on the floor.

"So be it," John said.

Mary touched John's arm. "Help me get him up on the bed."

John slid his hands under the Indian's shoulders, cradling his head between his forearms and Mary grabbed the Indian's feet. Together they lifted him onto the bed. Then John turned and walked back to the doorway. He pushed the door shut deliberately, but quietly. He took off his hat and placed it on one of the pegs beside the door, then took off his gun belt and hung it on a peg beside his hat.

John was more than a little uneasy at the thought of having a stranger share their home but found it not too difficult to accept when he thought of what his life would be like if the young Indian hadn't interceded on Mary's behalf.

On the morning of the fourth day the young warrior opened his eyes. He stared at the ceiling in bewilderment. He had never seen the inside of a white man's hogan and didn't recognize the lodge-pole pine stringers, or hand-sawn planking. Mary was boiling a grouse that Sam had shot at sunset the previous evening, preparing to make a grouse soup. She jumped when she heard the rustle of the blanket as the Indian threw the cover off. She stood high above him with a startled look on her face. He looked at her with questioning eyes, then tried to sit up. The stitches in his side pulled and the cracks in his ribs opened a little. The warrior let out a gasp and fell back down on the bed. The look on his face was that of a man who had just been smashed in the face by an unseen fist.

"You just lay back, now." Mary knelt beside the lean warrior. "You're pretty badly torn up and shouldn't be going anywhere just yet." She continued to jabber in a soft tone, trying to soothe the Indian's fears. "You took a nasty spill after you finished off the grizzly. You had a mighty large hole in your side, which I sewed up like a Thanksgiving Turkey's belly full of stuffing." She pulled back the edge of the part of the blanket that still covered him.

He looked down and grimaced. He had seen buffalo-hide hogan covers with better stitching, but of course, the edges of buffalo hides were cut rather than ripped. Seeing how badly he was hurt took the fight out of him and he laid back down, exhaled, and relaxed. He knew he wasn't going anywhere anytime soon.

Mary offered him a tin of water and he lifted his head eagerly. His mouth was as dry as last summer's smoked salmon, but he drank slowly. He wanted to show the white woman that he was a warrior—a man totally in control of his physical being. He sipped the water as nonchalantly as he would smoke his pipe in his own hogan. When he finished sipping the tin of water, she gave him another, and then another.

"You sure were thirsty." She had never been good at small talk. "I sure would be thirsty if I hadn't had anything to drink in as long as you haven't. I'll bet you're

THE CHINOOK RIVER PRINCESS

hungry, too. As soon as the canned carrots and beans cook a little, I'll give you a bowl of soup. Do you people eat soup? I guess not, but you probably have something like it; antelope stew, prairie dog chowder, or maybe even some squirrel bisque." She smiled warmly.

After ten minutes of sipping, he finally had his fill. He hadn't had any water in four days and was pretty well dehydrated.

She took a bowl from the cupboard and filled it from the steaming pot on the stove. Even though the aroma was driving the young warrior mad with desire, he remained as stoic as the cigar-store Indian that stood in front of Mr. Hawshorn's tobacco shop in Baltimore.

She knelt beside the young man and brought a spoon of broth to his lips. He opened his mouth a little, not knowing how he was to handle the white man's eating utensil. The broth was delicious, although he thought it could use a little sage seasoning like the women of his clan used. After patiently letting Mary feed him several spoons full, he turned on his side a little, lifted himself and rested on his left elbow. Then he reached out for the bowl. Mary gave it to him and he brought it to his lips to drink slowly. His eyes said thank you, even though his mouth remained mute.

"My name is Mary." She placed the flat of her right hand on her chest. "Mary. I'm Mary."

"Paw-tuk." He touched the lip of the bowl to his chest. "Paw-tuk."

"Pawtouch," she repeated.

He shook his head sternly. "Paw-tuk, Paw-tuk."

"Pawtuk?" She raised her eyebrows.

"Paw-tuk," he said, nodding.

As he slowly sipped the soup, Pawtuk cursed himself for having interceded on her behalf. If he had not, he realized, she would have been killed by the bear and he would be back among his own people. When the bear charged it was his instinct rather than his mind that directed his actions. His Grandfather asked for his pledge that he would not let the white woman kill anyone but he said nothing about keeping her alive.

Pawtuk put on about ten extra pounds eating Mary's cooking and was fit after only six weeks. Even though everyone at the ranch still wondered why he had been watching her, no one wondered any longer if his motives were bad.

When he had fully recovered, he returned to his position just inside the tree line. From there he maintained his surveillance. It was exactly as it was before, except that every day Mary took a plate of food out to Pawtuk, who would accept the offering without comment.

THE CHINOOK RIVER PRINCESS

Chapter 19

It was late-September, in the middle of the night, when Mary felt the first contraction. It frightened her. She wondered if she would die, like so many other women away from civilization, or be lucky enough to later feel the little thing suckling at her breast.

"John?" She spoke quietly, then shook him gently and spoke louder, "John?"

"What is it?" He quickly sat up in the bed and listened for sounds outside.

"I'm going to have the baby."

"Right now?" He threw back the covers and got to his feet.

"Not right this minute, but I'm starting to feel the baby trying to be born."

"I've got to get the doctor," he said, rushing around in the dark trying to locate the oil lamp.

There was a loud crashing sound, then he shouted, "Oh, damn!"

"What's going on, John?"

"I just fell over the chair."

"What are you doing?"

"I'm trying to find the damn lamp!"

"Are you all right?"

"Yeah, I'm fine. But I'll be finer if I can find the lamp."

"It's on the table. More over to your left."

He found the lamp and removed the chimney. The matches were on the table beside the lamp. The small flame seemed to light the whole room as John put the match to the wick. The glow on the top edge of the wick started to grow and within a few seconds, the room was flooded with yellow light.

"Well you'd better get your pants on and get moving. I don't want to have the baby before you get back."

"Don't you worry. I'll get back shortly, I promise."

He finally found his pants and shirt, got dressed, and then went to the bunkhouse. He woke Sam within five minutes of his getting out of bed.

"She's gonna have the baby soon, Sam. I think she'll be all right until I get back with the doctor, but if you hear something's wrong in there, see if you can help her, will you?"

"I wills, Mista John, you be sure o'that," Sam spoke with a conviction that caused the knots in John's stomach to ease.

John rode from the ranch house at breakneck speed. He'd have been killed if he hadn't known every inch of the road down the hillside because all he carried for light was an oil lantern with a back reflector. It cast a faint yellow glow only about ten feet in front of his horse. There was only a sliver of moon showing and beyond the range of his feeble light, the road appeared as a blue-black ribbon on a slightly lighter background.

It was just over an hour later that John reached Doc Pickard's place. He banged on the door frame for what seemed an eternity before Mrs. Pickard asked, "Who's there!"

THE CHINOOK RIVER PRINCESS

"It's John March, Martha. I need Doc right away. Mary's having the baby right now."

Martha opened the door. The lamp she was carrying blinded him. "Doc's not here, John." Her voice was dripping with regret. "He went to see to Old Man Fells before supper and's not back yet. He'll probably stay over and come back after sunup."

"Oh, no!" John reached out and grabbed Martha by the arm and shook her. "He's got to come," he spoke as if she could do something to bring the doctor home.

"He won't be home till late mornin', John."

"Then you come. You can help. I don't know nothin' about birthing' babies."

"I can't, John. I get sick at the thought of it, and I faint at the sight of blood."

"Well, what the hell am I supposed to do, damn it!"

"Maybe you could get Beth McGrath to help. She helped Doc deliver Meg Water's baby last year, and she said she helped a woman birth a baby when she lived back east."

Without another word, John bounded to his horse and rode off toward the McGrath's store.

"Beth, Beth!" He pounded on the kitchen window.

The racket roused Beth and Bret. Beth finally answered the door. "What's the matter, John?"

"Mary's having the baby and Doc's out at the Fells' place."

"What can I do?" she asked, somewhat perturbed.

"You can come back with me and help Mary get through this!"

"Well, you'll just have . . ." Beth stopped, sensing Bret's presence behind her. "All right, I'll go with you."

She wished that Bret weren't there. If he weren't, she'd have given John a piece of her mind.

"Good, I'll hitch up your buggy." John turned quickly and headed for the barn.

To John, it seemed an eternity before they were in the buggy, cutting through the darkness behind Bret's galloping roan gelding.

"You've got a lot of salt asking me to help deliver Mary's baby. If Bret weren't home I'd have told you to go to hell!"

John barely heard her over the clamor of the buggy wheels and the gelding's hooves impacting upon the rocky roadway.

John shouted to be heard, "I don't want to hear it!"

Beth became silent. If there had been more light, John would have seen her clenched jaw.

By the time they reached the turnoff to the ranch, the sky had lightened to a dark purple in the east, with just a hint of pink on the horizon. The buggy bounced and careened up the winding ruts toward the ranch house.

As the gelding's hooves slid to a stop in front of the hitching rail, John saw Sam and Clarence pacing in front of the house. They were afraid that entering would somehow violate the oldest and most sacred of female experiences.

"Is she all right, Sam?" John asked, as Beth climbed out of the buggy without help.

"I thinks so, Mista John. Miss Mary yelps lika hurt pup once t'wile, but I thinks her's alright."

Without saying a word, Beth climbed the five steps to the front door and entered.

Chapter 20

Mary was half-sitting and half-laying in bed when Beth came in. She was trying to contend with the wrenching throws of a contraction. The contraction eased in a few seconds and Mary fell back on the bed in exhaustion.

"Where's the doctor?" she asked, between gasps for air.

"The Doc is out at the Fells' ranch and won't be coming," Beth said it in a tone that would have been appropriate if Mary had asked what the weather was like outside.

"Oh no, what's going to happen to the baby?"

"It'll be fine. Babies are born all the time without doctors." Beth's tone was impatient and angry tone.

Mary couldn't understand why Beth would be angry, unless it was that she just didn't like being dragged out of her house in the middle of the night. Before she could think more about Beth's attitude, the grand-daddy of all contractions swept over her. It was as if she had a charlie-horse in the biggest muscle the world had ever known, and that muscle was located right in the middle of her body, attached to her pelvis. At times, she thought the pressure would push her pelvis right out onto the floor.

She screamed until there wasn't the least bit of air left in her lungs, then she mouthed a scream until she thought she would die from lack of air. At the moment she started to loose consciousness, the baby burst from her groin.

Her upper body fell back on the bed as her lungs refilled with the air she so badly needed.

Mary laid back on the sweat-soaked sheets for several minutes, gasping like a beached fish.

"Is it a boy?"

"Yes. It's a boy," Beth answered calmly.

"Why isn't it crying?"

"It hasn't started breathing yet," Beth spoke in the same tone that she would have said that the biscuits in the oven hadn't risen yet.

"Do something, don't just stand there looking at him!" Mary pushed herself up into a sitting position with her hands so that she could see the baby. "Do something. Damn it, Beth. Do something!"

"It's not for me to do. It's in God's hands." It was if Beth were only dreaming the events that were taking place.

Mary leaned forward and picked up the limp parcel laying between her spread legs and brought it to her chest, as if all it needed were nourishment. The child's skin had a slight blue-gray cast as it lay motionlessly on her breast.

"Oh God, do something," she pleaded, looking up at the ceiling.

Then she swung her legs over the edge of the bed and tried to stand. She was going to take the baby to John—he wouldn't let his baby die. Mary's legs buckled and she went down. She turned on her side in attempt to avoid landing on the baby. She hit the floor like a sack of potatoes thrown from the back of a buckboard. The baby fell from her arms, landing beside her. The newborn recoiled when it hit the hard, cold floor. Then he twisted and turned for a moment before sucking a lung full of air and screaming. Mary picked up her baby carefully and held it to her chest as she cried silently, her shoulders heaving.

"He should have been mine," Beth said angrily, after Mary had calmed.

"What?"

"He should have been mine. John should have given him to me, not you. John loves me. He loved me long before you came, and he loves me more than you."

Mary looked into Beth's eyes and saw that she was not sane at that moment. She knew that Beth had slipped over the edge of some precipice and was no longer in charge of her faculties. Her face was beet red and her eyes were opened wide, yet not seeing. She seemed to stare into nothingness.

"John loves me," Beth cocked her head to side as if she were listening for some sound outside. "After Anne died, I showed him how good it could really be with a woman—a woman who knew how to please a man like him. He wanted to marry me, but I wouldn't leave Bret. I was afraid. . . I was afraid that John would leave me someday, and I couldn't stand that. I love him too much. I'd die if he were to leave me."

Mary's head started spinning and everything seemed to move away from her, as if she were riding on the back of a wagon.

"Mary, Mary, are you all right?" John was shaking her shoulders. Then he picked her up and placed her back in bed, with the baby suckling at her breast.

"Where's Beth?" she asked as soon as she could speak.

"She left a few minutes ago." John furrowed his brow.

"Did she say anything?"

"Not a word. She just walked out to her buggy and rode off . . . that's when I came in and found you on the floor. What happened?"

"I don't know . . . I must have rolled out of bed," Mary tried to see something in John's face that belied Beth's claims to his love.

"He's beautiful." John leaning over and hugged her and the baby together.

"Yes, he is," she agreed, forgetting Beth for the moment and smiling down at the little fella they would name Matthew, after her father.

Mary rested quietly in bed for several days and Matt seemed to grow bigger minute by minute. Clarence catered to Mary as if she were his own little girl and cleaned and changed the baby regularly.

Mary had nothing to do but worry about what Beth had said. Could it be true . . . could John love Beth? When John is out in the hills all day tending the cattle, is he really? Or is he at McGrath's store—in the house behind the store, making love to Beth? No! It can't be, she assured herself. John loves me . . . maybe he was taken with her after Anne died, but now he loves me!

Day in and day out it was the same; she couldn't get Beth's claims out of her head. One moment she was sure that John was betraying her, the next moment she was sure he wasn't. Two weeks of torturing herself with doubts made her almost crazy with jealousy. It was after John had come to bed one night, three weeks after Matt was born, that she finally worked up the courage, or rather anger, to broach the subject. As they were lying quietly in bed, Mary tried to speak several times but couldn't make

THE CHINOOK RIVER PRINCESS

the words come out of her mouth. She lay in the dark, tears streaming from the corners of both eyes. On the fourth try, she finally forced the words to her lips. "Why didn't you tell me that you love Beth?"

John was silent for several moments. "What ever are you talking about?" He strained to control the panic he felt.

"The night Matthew was born Beth told me that you loved her and wanted to marry her."

John sighed as if he were exhaling out of his mouth everything that he was or ever would be. He was silent for more than a minute. "After Anne died . . . I didn't know what I'd do. Beth and Bret came by regularly, to see if they could help."

"Yes, I'll just bet!" Mary spit out the words.

"That's the way it was at first, then Beth started dropping by about lunch time, when I would come back to the house to get something to eat. She fixed my lunch once in a while . . . and one day she just hauled off and kissed me."

"I'll bet you just stood there and she attacked you, right?"

"One thing lead to another," he answered calmly, trying not to let Mary goad him into a fight, "and you can figure the rest."

"Does Bret know?"

"No."

"Did you ask her to marry you?"

"No."

"Well, she says that you did, but that she wouldn't leave Bret."

"That's a lie. I felt like an outlaw and I didn't want to hurt Bret. He's a good friend . . . I couldn't take his wife."

"No, you couldn't take his wife! I'll bet you had to force yourself just to mount her every day at lunch." She turned her back to him and cried. She cried as hard as she did when she lost her mother, father, little Josh and Jacob. It was several minutes before she calmed enough to hear John's words.

"Mary, I was very hurt and lonely when I did what I did. I don't expect that you'll ever forgive me for that, but you must know that I love you. I love you more than I have loved anyone or anything before. I'd die if anything happened to you, or if you left me."

She didn't reply and in a few moments felt the bed shaking gently. It was a few moments before she realized that he was crying. She didn't speak, but turned toward him and put her head on his quaking shoulder.

The next several days were difficult. Mary felt betrayed and couldn't feel the same unbridled love for John that she had before. John couldn't purge himself of the guilt that hung over him like a cloud. Each day was a little easier than the one before, and neither of them mentioned it again. Given enough time, the rift between them would heal.

One afternoon John spooked a bull grizzly from a stand of alder on a hill overlooking the ranch. He decided that it was time he taught Mary how to use a rifle. He didn't feel comfortable leaving her and Matt in the house without protection.

THE CHINOOK RIVER PRINCESS

John took her out behind the barn the next day and set up several bottles as targets. Mary learned quickly. After only a short briefing and a lot of practice, she could squeeze off some fairly good shots.

At one practice session John handed is 44-40 to Mary. "Here, I want you to try this."

"Why?"

"This hits a lot harder if you ever need to shoot a grizzly. I want you to know how it feels, just in case you need to shoot several times. If the first shot shook you up too much, you wouldn't get off a second shot."

"Will it hurt?" Took the rifle as if she weren't sure that she wanted it.

"It'll hit you pretty hard, but if you keep it tight to your shoulder it won't hurt too much."

"I'm not sure I want to do this."

"Yes you do. Now put up to your shoulder and pull it in tight," he instructed her.

Mary did as he said, pulling the rifle butt into her shoulder until it almost hurt. Then she squeezed the trigger until the hammer released. The rifle sounded like a cannon compared to the 30-caliber Winchester she'd been practicing with. The impact of the rifle butt on her shoulder pushed her back enough that she couldn't keep her feet.

Seeing her looking up at him with a wide-eyed expression on her face as she sat in the dirt was just too much, and John busted loose with a gut wrenching laugh he couldn't squelch. He laughed until he was limp with exhaustion and withered to the ground.

"Maybe I should just sit down before I shoot." She was staring up at John with a silly grin, "What do you think?"

The thought of Mary plopping herself down on her butt to draw a bead on a charging grizzly threw John into deeper fits, which finally washed over Mary as well. The two of them rolled in the dirt, laughing out all of the guilt and anger that had built up between them for so many weeks.

Pawtuk watched the couple's unusual antics from the crest of the hill behind the ranch house. He saw nothing funny in their actions. He was angry that they were playing games with a rifle that he would give his right arm to own. It was a weapon that would make him the most powerful warrior in his clan. He resented the white woman who, by her mere existence, kept him from his own people and his responsibilities as a warrior.

Chapter 21

Seven weeks after Matt was born, Beth stopped by the ranch for a visit, if one could call taking a twenty-mile buggy ride stopping by for a visit. Mary was hanging laundry when Beth's buggy crested the hill. She was more than a little surprised by the visit.

"Hello, Mary," Beth called before reining the gelding. "How do you like mothering?"

"It's fine." Mary was confused by Beth's good-natured banter. She had thought there would be a permanent abyss between them after what Beth had told her about John and herself.

"Great. I wanted to see the baby ever since Bret told me the good news."

"What good news?"

"What good news? Why the birth of course!" Beth furrowed her brow. "What's the matter with you, girl?"

"Well, you were here, Beth."

"Here when?"

"When Matt was born, of course."

"What are you and Bret up to?" Beth was starting to sound a little angry. "He said the same thing. You two make this up together?"

"We didn't make anything up."

"I don't want to hear anymore." Beth then smiled. "Where's that little one? I can't wait a second longer to see him!"

"He's asleep."

Beth's response was quick, "Well then, let's go in and wake him."

"He's beautiful," Beth squealed, picking Matthew out of the cradle Sam had built. She put the warm bundle to her shoulder. "He looks just like John."

As Beth cooed to Matt, patting him gently on the back, Mary put on a kettle of water for sassafras tea.

"That little thing eats like a horse," Mary complained. "I'm so sore, I can hardly stand it. I wonder if cows get sore." Mary set the cups of tea on the table. "Do you use sugar, Beth?"

"No, that's fine."

Beth continued to hold Matt as she sipped her tea. Mary noticed that her neck was starting to flush. "Are you getting too hot, holding Matt?"

"No, I'm fine."

Mary watched Beth carry on over Matthew, and as she did, she noticed that Beth's neck was turning a bright red, then almost purple. As she spoke, Beth's eyes became inflamed and almost angry looking, and her manner slowly changed. Before long, she started talking crazy, just as she did the night Matt was born.

"This is really my baby, you know." Beth looked down at Matt's sleeping form in her arms. "John worked it out. He knew I couldn't have one, so he sent for you so you could have it for me.

Mary turned a deathly shade of gray as the blood drained from her head. She stood and tried to take Matt from Beth.

"Don't touch him!" Beth ordered. "He's sleeping.

THE CHINOOK RIVER PRINCESS

Mary moved back to her chair and sat, afraid of what Beth might do to Matt if she got angry. She felt light-headed and her throat became instantly dry—so dry she couldn't have spoken even if she could have thought of something to say. She was scared, more scared than she had ever been—more than when the grizzly came after her.

"When John comes back, we're going to be leaving." Then Beth added, "We're going to move further up river.

Beth waited for Mary to speak, but Mary was silent.

"You'll move into the store with Bret. God wants it."

Mary finally croaked in disbelief, "God wants it?"

"Of course." Beth spoke in a patronizing tone, "God wants you to live with Bret and give him a son also."

The more Beth talked, the more frightened Mary became. It seemed as if a stranger had taken over Beth's body, and the stranger was talking absolute nonsense. Mary dug deep within herself for the strength to maintain her composure, then she filled beth's cup—the stranger's cup—with tea.

Mary sat quietly for almost an hour watching Beth rock Matt before she noticed Beth's neck becoming less flushed. Mary talked about her chores and anything else that she could think of except John, Matt or Bret, to take Beth's mind off the baby.

John and the hands returned about seven o'clock and by that time Beth had returned to being herself. She was acting perfectly normal and was perfectly delightful when the men came in from the hills.

"Hello, John," Beth said, as he sauntered in, removed his hat and placed it on the rack beside the door.

"Welcome, Beth. How do you like the newest March?"

"He's a fine boy, John. I'll bet you're awfully proud of him."

"You better believe it." John walked to Beth and took little Matt, to Mary's relief. "He's the finest young man born in these parts."

Beth left after a few more pleasantries. Mary almost collapsed from relief as Beth's buggy dropped out of sight over the crest of the hill. She tried to tell John what had happened with Beth earlier that afternoon before he and the hands returned from the outlying pastures, but he was not receptive.

"You're talking crazy, Mary. She must have been joking with you. You'll have to learn to know when she's joshin' you, and when she's serious."

"She was serious, John. You'd know it if you'd been here. You've got to believe me. I know what I'm saying."

"You're just upset about what I told you about what had been between us, but you've got to forget it. It doesn't matter now."

"That's not it, John. I tell you, before you came home she was as crazy as a one-legged cricket."

"Now, Mary, I don't want to have to tell you again . . . Beth's not crazy. She fools around sometimes, but that's just Beth. You'll just have to understand that."

Mary could see it was hopeless and dropped the subject. She knew the way Beth was acting when John came home would have convinced anyone that she was perfectly normal.

The next several days were a hell for Mary. She stayed in the house with the door bolted and prayed that Beth

THE CHINOOK RIVER PRINCESS

wouldn't return. She kept thinking of how her life had finally turned around and how happy she was living as Mrs. March. She also kept remembering how many times before she had been happy and how things had been taken from her—her mother, father, her home, little Josh, and finally Jacob. The more she remembered the more angry she became.

She knew that she had finally reached the point in her life where she had to do something to break the seemingly endless chain of tragedy that had plagued her. She had always been a victim of circumstance, and it was about to happen again. If she did nothing to stop her, Beth would ruin her life, just as it had been ruined so many times before. She didn't know how it would happen, but it surely would. She would loose John, or Matt, or the ranch or all of them if she didn't do something to stop it.

She told John of her fears, and again he concluded that Mary was being overly dramatic. Instead of being convinced that Beth was not normal, he was starting to believe that somehow the birth of Matt had affected Mary's mind. His efforts to console her only infuriated her and made her seem even more unstable.

Exactly two weeks after Beth's visit, Mary locked herself in the house as usual, after the men left to brand the cattle in the eastern pasture. She was preparing to dry some beans, when she heard a knock at the door.

"Who is it?" Mary was deathly afraid that it was Beth, or the stranger in Beth's body.

"It's me, Beth. I've come for my baby."

"Go away . . . he's not your baby, he's mine."

"You know that God wants me to have my baby, so give him to me, Mary. Don't make me have to do something I don't want to."

Mary was terrified. "Go away!" she screamed. "Go away!"

"I can't. You know I can't leave my baby."

"He's not yours, damn it. He's my baby and I won't let you hurt him."

"Hurt him? I could never hurt little John."

"Go home, Beth!" she screamed, as Matt began to bawl.

"You're hurting my baby, Mary. Don't hurt him please."

"I'm not hurting him. You're scaring him, Beth. Now go away."

"I won't go without Little John." Beth then fell silent.

Mary waited for Beth to speak again, but she waited in vain. Mary wondered what Beth was up to. She walked cautiously around on the first floor. She crept up to the edge of the window on the north side of the house. She peered uneasily around the rough hand-hewn logs that framed the window. She could see nothing but grass on the north slope behind and beside the house. She moved to the window on the east side of the house and as before could see nothing unusual. She made a full tour of the first floor, finishing up at the front door again. She put her ear to the door, listening for any evidence of Beth's presence.

There was a crash like a clap of thunder in Mary's ear and the door suddenly bowed inward an inch, hitting her cheek. Mary screamed when she saw the tip of an ax sticking through a newly opened crack in the door planks.

The top point of the axe blade slowly rocked as it disappeared back into the wooden plank. The door reverberated again, and the axe blade penetrated the door planks even further than it had before. The axe fell twice more upon the door before Mary was able to reach the rifle hanging on the wall beside the stove.

She opened the rifle's breach lock, just as John had showed her, and shoved in a 30-caliber cartridge. Then she slammed the breach closed. She turned the rifle upon the door, but hesitated. She couldn't fire. She was angry and scared enough to kill, but enough in control not to. She raised the rifle until it was pointing at the top of the door just below the upper sill and pulled the trigger.

Beth was standing to the side of the doorway so she could get a full swing with the axe. She brought the axe back as far as she could reach, preparing to slam the axe blade into the door with all of her strength. Just as she was about to bring her full weight to bear on the axe handle, a bullet tore a large hole through the top of the heavy door above her head. She stood in shocked disbelief for a moment, trying to understand what was happening. Inside, Mary heard a horse approaching at a gallop. Beth must have heard it also, because within seconds, Beth's buggy was retreating from the ranch house, darting down the rutted access road.

When Mary heard the lone horse come to a halt at the hitching rail, she pulled the door open and ran out. She expected to meet John. Instead, she found herself face-to-face with Pawtuk. He stared at her for a moment, as the sound of Matt's screaming came from the open door washed around them and then was absorbed into vast landscape.

Pawtuk showed no emotion. He turned his horse and guided it in a slow walk back toward the trees. Mary was sure it was Pawtuk, rather than her shooting, that scared Beth off. She wondered why he had waited until she fired the rifle before coming. She couldn't imagine that he hadn't heard Beth beating on the door with the ax, since he was always close by.

Mary told John when he returned what had happened that day. Upon seeing the damaged door, he immediately remounted his horse and raced toward McGrath's store.

It was several hours before John returned. He entered slowly, and said nothing.

"Well, what happened, John?"

"Beth wasn't out here today. She spent the morning putting goods on the shelves, then went out to pick blackberries and to visit Mrs. Hall. It must have been someone else." He was sure that Mary had damaged the door herself.

"Someone else? Someone else! It was Beth, I talked to her through the door."

"If it was Beth, why didn't you open the door?"

"Beth wants to take Matt. I'm afraid she'll hurt him."

"Damn it, Mary," he cursed through his clenched teeth. "Beth won't hurt Matt, what's the matter with you?"

"She was here!" Mary wanted desperately to be believed. "Why don't you believe me?"

"I don't know what's happened to you. Ever since Matt was born, you haven't been yourself. Sam says that he's seen it happen before. Sometimes a woman gets upset from havin' a baby. He says you'll get over it."

"Sam said that?" Mary stood in stunned disbelief. "Sam doesn't believe me?"

THE CHINOOK RIVER PRINCESS

"It's not a matter of believing you. You aren't well."

Mary could suddenly see the futility of her position and acquiesced. "Maybe you're right. I've been awfully tired . . . and I have bad dreams."

"I'm sure you'll get over it." He took her in his arms and then stroked her hair as her head rested on his shoulder.

"I guess you're right," she sighed, "I think I just need some rest."

John stayed at the house with Mary for three days, which was all the time he could spare away from his chores. In those three days he saw Mary begin to relax. She became more like the woman he had married and less like the maniac he'd been living with for the past several months. On the fourth day he returned to ranching, confident in her swift recovery.

Chapter 22

Mary saddled her horse just after sunrise. After tightly cinching the saddle's girth, she slid the thirty-caliber rifle into the saddle scabbard. She placed her left foot in the stirrup and pulled herself up and onto the saddle. She turned the mare out of the barn and rode past the house. She turned onto the pathway that skirted the hills as it made its way to the river below and dug her heels in the mare's ribs.

John and the hands had left about a half-hour before. She was sure they were well away and wouldn't see her leave. She had fed Matt and put him down to sleep. If she were lucky, she could be back before his next feeding.

The ride was agony. The thoughts of what lay ahead weighed heavily on her. The hour-and-a-half ride gave her too much time to contemplate her scheme. She vacillated between turning back or continuing on. One moment she thought she couldn't go through with it, and the next she was determined, remembering how Beth had come after Matt.

Remembering the panic she felt for Matthew's safety brought bile up in her throat. It was maternal instinct that kept her moving toward the McGrath's store. It was stronger than her aversion for what she had to do.

What had Jacob said, as they sat by the smoldering fire on the plains? "You could kill if the price were high enough?" She had been so sure he was wrong. She wondered if Jacob would agree that the price was high enough. Her belief in Jacob's endorsement —the endorsement of his ghost—was vital. John would never agree that killing another was justified—he was too sure that the world conformed to his image of what it should be. In his world, people are who they pretend to be.

When she reached the last turn of the river, just upstream of the McGrath's place, Mary turned the mare away from the stream bank and the old girl labored up the slope. Mary forced her to climb, without rest, until they were well within the trees. Then she turned the mare west again, to circle behind the store. She rode within a finger of trees that stretched from high on the mountainside down to within thirty yards of Beth's back door. She dismounted and tethered the mare in a dense thicket about ten yards inside the outer edge of the woods.

Mary pulled the rifle from its scabbard. The air was still and the sun was high in the crystal blue sky. She looked up through the pine needles, into the sun. If, at that moment, she had seen a sign, any kind of sign, she would have gladly abandoned her plan, but she saw no sign. She let the rifle rest in the crook of her elbow and walked a few yards between and around the large pines toward the house. The pine needles on the ground were deep and her steps were comfortably quiet. She knelt behind a rock that rose about two and a half feet above the surrounding soil. Then she moved her torso to the side and lowered her left hip to the ground. In a sitting position, she rested the rifle barrel on the right side of the boulder. There, she waited, her mood continuing to cycle between firm resolve and panicked despair.

She was unaware that Pawtuk had followed. He sat silently on his horse only forty yards away. He watched for several minutes until he was certain of her intent. He quietly dismounted, holding the new lance he fashioned to replace the one he destroyed when he killed the grizzly. He slipped up to within fifteen feet of where she sat. He stood in silence.

It was about a half-hour later that Beth came out of the back door. Mary was thinking of what she might fix for supper and was caught totally off guard. Beth came out quickly and was about ten feet away from the house before the door's rope and counter weight pulled the door shut with a loud slam. Mary was startled to attention as Beth walked toward her. Beth carried a basket of rubbish to contribute to the trash pit, which was about ten yards from the edge of the woods.

Mary pulled the rifle butt firmly into her shoulder and sighted down the rifle barrel. The vertical blade of the front sight was centered in the notched rear sight, and superimposed on the middle of Beth's chest. The blade of the front sight seemed to dance in small circles on Beth's chest as her bouncy gate brought her closer, but the sight never strayed from its fatal mark. Mary slowly pulled the hammer back as she waited for Beth to get closer. Pawtuk cocked his arm, preparing to loose the lance in an instant. From where he stood, he could see Mary's trigger finger resting beside the trigger on the trigger guard.

Nervous sweat beads rolled down Mary's brow, momentarily blinding her. She quickly wiped the salty water from her right eye. When she looked back again, she had lost her sight picture and had to re-sight on the approaching figure. When she was sure that Beth was too

THE CHINOOK RIVER PRINCESS

close to miss, she tired to raise her finger to the trigger, but couldn't. Her finger wouldn't obey her command. It refused to move. Jacob had been wrong. The rifle butt slipped from her shoulder. Her body went limp all of her weight shifted to the left, her left shoulder resting against the rock. She wept silently in relief.

Beth tossed the rubbish into the grave-sized hole. She then turned and walked back to the house, as oblivious to her brush with death as Mary was to her own. Pawtuk relaxed the grip on his lance and then, as silently as he had come, slipped back through the pines.

As Mary crested the hill in front of the house, she could hear Matt screaming to be fed. She rode into the barn and quickly unsaddled her horse. She carried the rifle back to the house and placed it back over the mantle. She then pulled off her boots and went eagerly to the task of feeding Matt. Whenever Matt started crying she felt a stirring in her breasts and shortly thereafter, if she didn't suckle him, her blouse would be wet with milk.

As Matt gorged himself at her breast, Mary wondered what was going to become of them. She thought of packing some clothes for herself and Matt and taking the buggy, but where would she go? She knew no one well enough to impose upon, and she couldn't tell anyone what she was running from. They, whoever they might be, wouldn't believe her anymore than John did. If she were back in Baltimore she could go to Father O'Brien.

That's it, she thought, I'll go to see the preacher that married us . . . Reverend Walsh.

She tried to remember where he lived. "Fifteen miles up river," he had said.

Matt finished and fell asleep in her arms. After a few minutes, the soreness in her breasts eased and she relaxed into the rocking chair. She dozed off. She dreamed of her life in Baltimore before her mother died.

THE CHINOOK RIVER PRINCESS

Chapter 23

The morning sun had just crested the eastern ridge of the river canyon and was casting long shadows when Mary turned the buggy onto the narrow road that followed the Chinook River upstream. Matt was sleeping restlessly in a small crate resting under the buggy seat, along with Mary's rifle. She had packed the crate with cloth scraps so he wouldn't get hurt from the jostling he was sure to get on the rough road.

She left a note on the table for John so he wouldn't worry. The buggy was about seven miles upstream by the time the sun had risen forty degrees in the eastern sky. The terrain grew more rugged as she followed the river toward its headwaters. The rolling hills gave way to steep rock walls, which came down almost to the river's edge. The roar of the river was deafening as it crashed through the rocky channel.

By noon the narrow road had turned into not much more than a foot path and she was ready to give up and head back.

Surely, she thought, a preacher wouldn't live out here. There's no one out here to minister to.

As she drove on looking for a spot to turn the buggy, she noticed a narrow foot-worn trail that branched off to the right of the main path. It ran beside a creek and into the trees that lined the bottom of a small canyon. She turned onto the trail, preparing to turn around, and caught a glimpse of a small house behind a stand of cottonwoods.

Instead of turning, she headed toward the house. As she drew close, she could see that it was rather unkempt and appeared deserted. She brought the buggy to a halt in front of the small shanty. She climbed down from the buggy and tethered the horse to the unpainted porch post. Then she took Matt from his comfortable crate bed under the seat. She walked around the side of the house calling, "Is anyone here?"

"Hello," came an answer. A curious, unshaven man rounded the corner of the house.

"I was looking for the minister's home." Mary hoped the man was familiar with the pastor.

"Well, you found it, Miss. . . why it's Mrs. March, isn't it?" He offered his hand.

"Mr. Walsh?" Mary asked in disbelief.

"Yes, it is I. Most people don't recognize me when they see me in my element. I wish you'd call me Nim rather than Mr. Walsh."

"Nim?"

"Yes, Nim. It's short for Nimrod."

"Why are you out here? Where's your congregation?"

"I have no congregation, Mrs. March."

"How can a minister not have a congregation to minister to?"

"I'm not a practicing pastor anymore, my dear."

"Not a practicing minister?"

"Now don't look so upset." He noticed the panicked look on her face. "Don't you fret, you *are* married to Mr. March. I'm still an ordained minister of God—I just don't have a regular congregation. I only perform

THE CHINOOK RIVER PRINCESS

ceremonies because there isn't another man of the cloth for several hundred miles."

"Oh." Mary's relief was evident.

"Come up on the porch and sit awhile." He extended his arm in the direction of the front of the house. "I'd ask you in, but the air circulation is mighty poor in there. It gets mighty hot."

"Well, thank you, Nim. I'd like to sit a spell and talk if you don't mind."

"Not at all, Mrs. March."

"If I'm going to call you Nim," she smiled and tossed her head to get the hair out of her face, "then you're going to have to call me Mary."

"Very well, Mary," he offered her a weathered rocker, then pulled a straight-back chair out a little from the front wall for himself.

"How'd you like a cup of cold water? I just brought a fresh bucket from the spring."

"Thank you, Nim. Do you mind if I feed Matthew? He hasn't eaten in several hours."

"No, I don't mind at all." It was a lie. He was always ill at ease whenever a woman nursed in front of him.

Mary put Matt's head under the bottom edge of her shirt in such a way that Matt could feed easily and Mr. Walsh wouldn't see her breast.

Nim was visibly agitated, even though Mary made every attempt to put him at ease. He was angry with himself for not being able to control his emotions. A woman nursing her young was the most natural act of being human and should be regarded as such. Even so, he found it impossible to accept the act for what it was. It must be my puritanical upbringing, he thought.

Mary was a stunning woman and, even though she was wearing one of John's shirts, Nim found her exceptionally arousing. Her long hair draped her shoulders like a silk shawl and the nipple of her left breast pushed gently against the inside of her shirt. He could plainly see that there was a fabulous female body under the ill-fitting shirt. He sat quietly and watched until he could stand it no longer.

"You must be famished." He got to his feet. "I forgot how late it is. I'll make us something to eat."

"Oh no. Don't on my account."

"Well, on my account then. I'm starved and I eat alone too often to let you get away without joining me."

"Of course. I'd love to join you."

"You just keep right on with what you're doing and I rustle up something in a jiffy." His cheeks were brightly flushed.

As she rocked on the porch with Matt pulling on her breast, she wondered how John would react to her note. He would most certainly come after her, but would he come in anger or understanding? He'll be angry, she finally concluded.

The hollow was much different than her home on the hillside. There was no breeze and it was strangely quiet. She could see no hawks overhead and there were no birds playing in the Cottonwood trees. The only sound was that of water babbling over the rocks in the creek bed as it moved toward the river. She relaxed for the first time since Beth defiled her home. She felt safe. Beth couldn't get to her here. She couldn't violate the sanctuary of this dilapidated house in the cottonwoods.

THE CHINOOK RIVER PRINCESS

It was about a half-hour before Nim reappeared in the rustic hand-hewn, pine-framed doorway.

"Here you go, Mary." He handed her a bowl of warm beans and a slab of cold cornbread.

"Oh, thank you." She was grateful for the trouble he had gone to.

"It's just something I had left from supper last night. I hope it's all right."

"It's wonderful," she said, smiling warmly. She ate slowly, realizing it was a special meal—a meal prepared by a man of god. It symbolized security in a world of distrust, doubt, and danger.

"It's delicious," she kept repeating, as she ate. After several minutes of silence, she said, "You must be an accomplished cook."

"Not at all. That is, not with other foods. Beans is my speciality. I can make beans taste pretty good. I eat them almost every meal—not by choice of course."

"They taste like none I've ever had." She tried to discern the myriad of tastes that complimented the nutty beans.

"I put in some herbs that grow along the creek and some of the red fruit that grows on vines along the tree line. The Indians call the fruit *tommas*."

"Well, these beans are magnificent."

"Thank you." Nim beamed with delight.

"Are you married, Nim?"

"Not so you'd notice." He looked uneasily down at his hands, which he rubbed together slowly.

"I'm sorry. I shouldn't have asked."

"No, don't be sorry. It does me good to talk about it every so often. It was five years ago, or was it six . . . I forget. Anyway, Laura, that's her name, up and left. I had a parish in a small town about sixty miles east then. I don't know why she left, but she did. Maybe she just couldn't take living out here any longer. She missed the east as soon as we crossed the hills west of the Shenandoah. She never seemed to get used to being out here."

"I can understand that." Mary nodded knowingly. "The land is so big you feel alone and overwhelmed by it."

"Could be. I think that's why I took over this house. Here, snuggled away in this draw, the world doesn't seem so big."

"You're right about that. It seems so cozy and friendly here. I feel I could stay forever."

"Feel free. I could surely use the company."

"Oh, I can't stay too long. I just needed to get away for a rest."

"You will stay a little while, won't you?"

"I'll stay a bit, until I figure out what I'm going to do."

"There's a breeze starting to blow up the canyon," Nim said with satisfaction. "It always starts about this time every day this time of year."

"It feels heavenly." The breeze gently teased the hair draping her shoulders.

"We can go inside now if you like, Mary. The breeze will cool off the house."

"I should put Matt down for a nap if you have somewhere that I can lay him down."

"You can put him on the bed by the back window. It won't be too hot there."

THE CHINOOK RIVER PRINCESS

Mary put Matt down on the bed as Nim suggested and laid down beside him. She was exhausted and dozed off almost as soon as her eyelids touched.

Mary had been lying on her stomach sound asleep just before she pushed herself up with her hands, raised her head and quickly looked around the room. Her heart was racing and she was covered in cool damp sweat. It took her several seconds to get her bearings. She had been terrified by something in her dream, but the memory dissipated like smoke on a breezy day. She looked at Matt. He was sleeping soundly, even though the sun was shining on the bed where he lay. Out of the corner of her right eye, she saw movement. She looked quickly at the grimy window panes, but saw nothing.

From where he sat, Nim could see Mary on the bed.

"Are you all right?" he asked.

"Yes, I'm fine. I was just dreaming. How long have I been asleep?"

"If you went to sleep right after you laid down, you've had about three hours."

"That was rude of me." Mary was embarrassed.

"Not at all. You obviously needed the rest."

"I guess I did." Stretched her arms back.

"Who's Beth?" Nim asked, as he stood at the stove stirring a pot.

"Beth?"

"Yes. Is that Beth McGrath?"

"What do you mean?"

"Several times you said, 'Beth' in your sleep."

"I don't know what I was dreaming. It might have been Beth McGrath. What else did I say?"

"Nothing. Just Beth."

"Are you cooking again, Nim?"

"I'm just warming up some more beans for supper."

"Great!" Mary put her hands together as if preparing to give thanks. "I could stand another helping of your beans and now's the prefect time since Matt's still asleep."

"You say that now, but I bet it shan't be long before the smell of beans will make you gag your toenails up."

"That'll be the day." She laughed.

Before she'd finished chuckling there was a rap at the door.

"I wonder who that'd be," Nim headed for the door,. "I haven't had company in months and today I get two visits."

Mary was sure it was John. She didn't expect that he would get back to the ranch house before dark, but he must have gone home early for some reason and found her note.

When Nim swung the door open Mary's breath caught in her throat.

Chapter 24

"Beth, Beth McGrath," Nim stepped back from the open door a little, "Well come on in."

"Thank you, Mr. Walsh."

"Please, Beth. Call me Nim."

"What brings you here, Beth?" Mary asked, afraid of what her answer would be.

"I went by the house and found your note." She reached in her dress pocket and producing the crumpled piece of paper.

Mary's heart fell. John wouldn't see the note and wouldn't be coming.

"So you came out to say hello?" Mary asked.

"I came out to get my baby!" Beth shouted.

Nim stepped back a few steps in confusion.

"Did you think you could get away with my baby?" Beth's voice cracked with emotion as her neck turned a deep red.

"I just came out to visit Mr. Walsh."

"You lie. Your note said that you had to get away. It said that you were afraid of me. Why are you afraid. Are you afraid I'll take my baby?"

"It's not your baby, Beth," Nim interjected in a confused tone as if he weren't really sure.

"It is my baby! So I'm going to have to kill you too?" She grabbed the long-bladed kitchen knife that rested in a slot on the cutting board and turned on him. The raised blade came down in a flash, slipping easily between his ribs and puncturing his heart. He let out a grunt of disbelief and stood unmoving for a few moments. Beth then raised the knife out of his chest in a mirrored motion of the thrust. This death would go unrecorded by the ring, not being Mary's doing, but from his position in the corner of the room, the Dark Angel couldn't help smiling.

Beth turned on Mary. Her lunge just grazed Mary's shoulder as Mary threw herself past Beth and rushed for the doorway. Beth rushed after her. Mary didn't stop on the porch, but bounded down the steps to her buggy. Nim had unhitched her horse and had tethered it to a small tree beside the porch, but luckily he hadn't moved the buggy. Mary bounded to the buggy in three massive strides and reached under the seat. At first she didn't feel the rifle, but her fingers played over the boards that formed the bed of the storage bin until they touched the smooth steel of the barrel. She heard Beth's rapid footsteps on the porch and then stairs. She pulled the rifle clear of its resting place as she heard Beth's button-top shoes hit the hard-packed dirt at the bottom of the porch steps. Mary pushed the lever down and forward with her left hand as she started to turn. She had brought the lever back up by the time she faced Beth.

"Don't come any closer, Beth."

Beth didn't answer, but she slowed to a walk. She acted as if Mary were just any other person she was approaching to greet. From her actions, Mary could have thought that Beth bore her no ill will, but she knew better. Beth raised the knife above her right ear.

"Don't come any closer, Beth, or I'll shoot!"

THE CHINOOK RIVER PRINCESS

Beth acted as if she didn't hear a thing. She kept coming as Mary raised the rifle to her shoulder.

"Stop! Don't come any closer!" Mary gripped the rifle more tightly, placing her finger on the trigger.

Mary hesitated as long as she dared, then tightened her grip on the trigger. Before the rifle could fire, Mary saw a flash of movement coming from her right. In an instant Beth was laying at her feet, Pawtuk's spear protruding from her left temple. Pawtuk was silent as he walked up to Beth's limp body and retrieved his lance.

Darkness came quickly, so Mary invited herself to share the fire that Pawtuk made for himself just outside of the stand of cottonwoods. She fed Matt as she studied the Indian's emotionless face in the flickering firelight.

"Why did you kill her?" She posed the question as if he would understand her words. "Why didn't you kill her earlier? Why did you wait until just the instant before I pulled the trigger? You could see that I was going to do it, so why didn't you just let me?"

He didn't react to her words. If he had understood her language he would have said, 'I was waiting to see if she could kill you so I could go home. I only killed her so you would not.' Of course he didn't understand, so he remained in his squatting position, tossing small sticks into the fire.

His thoughts were of his tribe. Oh how he longed to share his grandfather's fire. How long will this white woman live? he wondered. At the time he didn't understand the mission to which his grandfather had committed him; he merely accepted its importance to their tribe, past and present. He couldn't help wondering how long before the red-eyed serpent on her finger slithered away on its belly and he could go home.

The Angel of Light arrived to find the Dark Angel watching Mary and Pawtuk from the darkness beyond the light of the fire.
"What is it that you want now?" She thought he might be angry.
"You interfered!" He was clearly angry. "She would have killed her had he not done it first, and you put him up to it." He pointed his long-nailed finger at the young warrior. "The death should count, as it would have if you hadn't interfered."
"I interfered?" She smiled sweetly, raising her left eyebrow. "And who was it who caused the hawk to dislodge the rock, making Jacob fall to his death so that Mary would not be diverted from this meeting this day?"
"You ruined it! The death should be on Mary's head."
"No!" She was firm. "Beth's death is on yours."
"You caused him to kill Beth!" He pointed again at Pawtuk. "The death should count for me."
"I did nothing but let one man glimpse his destiny and he pledged his grandson's life to balance the scales. Our agreement was that mankind, through the ring, would determine its own destiny. I did nothing more than allow it to be so."

The next day, John was pensive as he drove Mary home in the surrey. The hot sun was beating down on him from the left side as Mary suckled Matt in the shade of the surrey's top.

THE CHINOOK RIVER PRINCESS

John was silent the entire trip back until the carriage started the climb from the river. "I can hardly believe what Beth did and I'm so sorry that I didn't believe you all along. I couldn't blame you if you decided to leave me and go back to Baltimore."

"I have no life in Baltimore. My whole world is here." Mary was silent a moment and then added, "I feel like I was hanged and at the last second, someone cut the rope. I can't believe I'm still alive and still have Matt. I'm so relieved that I can forgive you anything."

"Thank God. I don't know if I could go on without you."

Mary leaned her head against John's shoulder and sobbed, "Let's go home."

John helped Mary get down from the carriage, then he stood by the horse's shoulder as Mary went in the house. He walked the horse to the barn, unhitched her, put her in her stall, shut the gate, and sat down heavily on the hay-strewn dirt floor. He hung his head and sighed. He asked himself how he could have forsaken Mary's claims and scorned her fears for her own life, and the safety of their son? How could he have had more faith in Beth? "I will never doubt her again!"

Chapter 25

The new land was good for Sam. For the first time in his life, he was truly free and happy. He was a respected ranch hand who was allowed to make decisions about how he did his work and how he would live his life. Being with men who spoke not correct English but a much more grammatical English had improved his mastery of the language, and just speaking more like other freemen made Sam more accepted by those he met and worked with.

His relationship with Mary had changed after she married but that was to be expected. He didn't resent her being less dependent on him. He understood she now had Mr. March to talk to about the things that troubled her, and about her aspirations and dreams.

One day, John asked Sam to go to Kester's general store to pick up ten rolls of barbed wire. Bret McGrath sold the store to Steve and Marsha Kester after Beth died. He had to sell out because there were just too many years of memories piled on the store shelves and in the wardrobes in the house out back.

Sam pulled the wagon to a stop in front of the store. When he climbed off the seat, it creaked and squeaked with relief. Sam was a much bigger man than the buckboard seat was sprung for. He tied the team to one of the hitching posts. He removed his hat and beat it on his

THE CHINOOK RIVER PRINCESS

thigh to get the dust out of the felt before he entered. It was cool inside.

"Afternoon, Sam."

"Afternoon, Mr. Kester."

"It's mighty hot out there isn't it?"

"It shore is."

"Help yourself to some water." Steve nodded toward the unglazed red-clay water pot hanging from a rafter near the back door. The water soaked the porous pot and it's constant evaporation in the dry air kept it almost twenty degrees cooler than the air outside.

"Thank ya, Mr. Kester, I appreciate it."

Sam walked to the back of the store, lifted the ladle off the nail in the post, dipped it in the pot and took a drink. He smiled broadly and Steve thought it was because the water was so cool. The water was mighty cool and Sam appreciated the fact, but much more, he appreciated how different it was out west where a black could drink from a ladle that white men used. He refilled the ladle and was taking another long drink when, though the open back door, his eyes fixed on a woman hanging clothes. She was dark, but not as dark as he. She was thin and tall, her hair long and curly. She looked almost black, but at the same time not black. She had a familiar look, like that of the Indians back at the camp where he and Mary had been held captive. She stood as if she owned the breeze that was blowing the shirt she was pinning to the clothesline.

"Who's the lady out back?" Sam asked.

"That's Keewa. We hired her to work in the store and to help Marsha with the chores around the house.

"Where she from?"

"She was living at the Mission down river. The mission took her in after her mother died."

"How'd she die?"

"Got the fever last winter."

"She looks kinda black."

"Her father was a buffalo soldier. He stayed in the area after his enlistment was up. Her mother was an Indian."

"What kind Indian?"

"What do you mean what kind?"

"What tribe did she belong to?"

"How would I know? An Indian's an Indian."

Sam hung the ladle back on its nail on the post. The water didn't seem as fresh and cool as it did at first taste.

"Mr. March needs ten spools of wire."

"Is that all?"

"That's all he said."

"Well, you just pull the buckboard around back by the storage shed and I'll load you up."

"Thanks, Mr. Kester."

After the wire was all loaded, Sam drove the wagon around to the east side of the store. It was a bit longer distance than going back the way he had come but it took him close to the clothesline. Keewa was carrying the empty laundry basket to the back door of the house. She looked up as he drove by. He grasped his hat by the crown, lifting it several inches above his head as he passed. He smiled. "Good afternoon, Miss Keewa."

Keewa didn't acknowledge him for a moment. She had a quizzical look, as if she hadn't understood him. Sam kept his hat off until she nodded.

THE CHINOOK RIVER PRINCESS

All the way back to the ranch, Sam hummed a tune he had heard the boat wrights sing as they hammered jute into the hulls of the ships in drydock.

Chapter 26

Several days later, Sam offered to go to the store to pick up the groceries for Clarence and Clarence was more than willing to pass the chore to Sam.

Sam walked into the store more quickly than he usually did and smiled when he saw Keewa behind the counter cutting some printed cotton fabric for Mrs. Talbot. He examined the tools on a table in the center of the store, waiting for Mrs. Talbot to finish her shopping.

When she had gone, Sam walked to the counter. "This here's a list of what Mr. Clarence needs, Miss Keewa."

"Why didn't Clarence come? He always picks up the groceries."

"I think he has somethin' more 'portant ta do."

"What's more important than a cook buying his groceries?"

"I doan know, Miss Keewa."

"Why do you call me Miss Keewa, instead of Keewa, or Miss Russel?"

"I doan know, Miss Keewa. Back east weze always call ladies by their given names, an' Miss."

"Who's we? I've known men from the east before. They didn't call me Miss Keewa."

"We blacks"

"Just blacks?"

"Yes."

"Why?"

THE CHINOOK RIVER PRINCESS

"I doan rightly know, Miss Keewa."

"You can call me Keewa, or Miss Russel, but don't call me Miss Keewa. It sounds stupid and you don't look like a stupid man."

"Yes, Ma'am."

"And don't Ma'am me. I must be fifteen years younger than you."

"Yes, Ma'am . . . I mean Miss Russel."

"I'll have this order ready in 'bout a quarter hour. Why don't you go outside and have a smoke while you wait?"

"I don't smoke but I'll be outside if you want."

"I don't want you outside. I just thought you would get bored waiting in here. I thought you might want a smoke. Mr. Kester doesn't allow no smoking in the store . . . could start a fire."

"I wait here, if you doan mine."

"I don't mind, Mr. Grande."

"How'd you know my name?"

"I asked Mr. Kester when you were here last time. Now stop talking to me. If you keep talking, I'll never get your order right."

"Yessem . . . I mean Keewa. I'll stop talking an' let ya work, if you call me Sam."

She smiled warmly. "All right then, Sam."

Sam did all of Clarence's grocery shopping and picked up all the hardware from Kester's store after that. Whenever Keewa wasn't working and Sam had free time from his duties at the ranch, the buckboard could be found several miles upriver, parked beside a big stand of birch.

There was a brook running through the birch and the birch woods made a cool place to picnic.

On Sundays, Sam ate dinner with Mary, John, and little Matt. The dinners were the only way Mary could think of to keep in touch with Sam. She had a husband and son, but Sam was the only family ties she had to her old world and she didn't want to lose all ties to that world. Sam was her anchor in a new and tempestuous sea of experiences.

John said grace as Matt pounded on his high-chair table with his spoon. Mary put the palm of her left hand under Matt's spoon and said in a whisper, "Don't do that, honey," but he moved the spoon to the side so he could get a good report from the table top.

When John finished the prayer, Sam spoke up, "It looks mighty good, as always, Miss Mary."

Mary smiled brightly. "Just a simple stew."

"Your stew's always mighty good."

"Mary always sets a fine meal," John added.

"That's shore 'nuff a fact, Mr. March."

"Speaking of cooking, Sam, is Keewa a good cook?"

"She shore is, Mr. March. You should taste her pies."

"I'd like to. She can bake me one anytime."

"I'll have her make you a sour cherry pie. It'll be a best you ever ate."

"If she wanted to make you a pie, John, she would have done it. Don't have Sam twist her arm."

"If Sam wants to twist her arm, let him."

"I don't want you putting a strain on their relationship. Next thing, you'll be asking Sam to have her do your laundry."

"I wouldn't do that and you know it."

"He couldn't hurt our 'lationship, Miss Mary. We're gonna get married."

Mary was surprised at the sudden revelation. She was happy for Sam, but fearful for what it might mean to their relationship.

"Congratulations, Sam. This calls for a celebration." John got up and went to the corner cupboard. "This calls for some sherry." He opened the cupboard door and took out a bottle of sherry and three small glasses.

"I didn't even know you were courting the young woman." Mary looked hurt.

"Weeze been seein' each other for almost five months now."

"How come I didn't know?"

John was pouring a small glass of sherry for her. "I guess you just don't see the right people. Sam and Keewa have been the talk of the bunkhouse for months now."

"Well, I don't get to spend much time with the hands in the bunkhouse."

"That's true," John looked uneasy, "I forget that you don't have as much opportunity to chat with others."

Matt hit his table with the spoon again.

Mary slapped his hand, "I said not to do that! Now stop it!"

Matt pouted a few seconds and then started bawling. John gave Mary a hard look.

"I told him not to do it." Mary took the napkin off her lap. She stood up and threw the napkin down on the table. She returned John's hard look and then turned and hurried into the kitchen.

John looked at Sam, cocked his head to the side, raised his eyebrows and then went back to eating. Matt quieted down after about thirty seconds.

"Where are you going to live, Sam?"

"When?"

"After you and Keewa get married?"

"I doan know. I been savin' most all you paid me, 'cep what I spend for clothes. Maybe someday I have enough to buy a small piece a land."

"You'll need a place to live till then. Keewa can't live in the bunkhouse with you. That'd be improper."

"She'll juss have to live at Kestor's like now and I'll stay in the bunkhouse."

"That's no way to start a marriage."

"No choice, Mr. March. We'll be all right."

Mary caught just the end of the conversation as she came back from the kitchen. She sat down and put her napkin back in her lap and tried to press the wrinkles out of it. "We'll be all right about what, Sam?"

"Keewa and I be all right. She'll keep working and living at Kestor's and I'll stay in the bunkhouse."

"Nonsense, Sam. A man and wife can't live apart, it's not Godly. You'll just have to put off the wedding until you can afford a place of your own."

"It would take him years to save enough for a place of his own, Mary."

Sam and John were silent though the rest of the meal and Sam left soon after they finished eating. He usually sat on a stool in the kitchen and talked with Mary as she washed the dishes after a meal, but this time he was quick to leave.

THE CHINOOK RIVER PRINCESS

John came into the kitchen and stood behind her as she did the dishes. "Why were you so hard on Sam today?"

"I don't know. I didn't mean to be."

"You were a bit short with him."

"Oh, no. I guess it's because Sam's been with me all my life and I couldn't stand to lose him."

"You wouldn't lose him. You don't have him now—he's just a good friend. He'll always be a good friend, unless you push him away."

"Oh, John. Tell me when I'm acting like an idiot toward Sam. I don't want to push him away."

"I'll let you know when you're being too hard on him."

Several days later, Sam and John were clearing rocks that had fallen into the Whiskey Creek irrigation ditch.

"I have a business proposal for you, Sam. I think it'll solve your problem of having no place to live with Keewa."

"I'm lisnin', Mr. March. Keewa is getting anxious to get married, and she doesn't want to live at Kester's no more."

"The Sheridan place across the river isn't doing well and Sheridan is about ready to sell out. I don't have any land across the river because it's too hard to get to during the spring floods. I can't have crops and cattle I can't get to for six or eight weeks. If you were living across the river, you could take care of things when the river's up."

"You'll let me live at the Sheridan place if I keep it runnin' for ya?"

"More than that. I don't need another ranch house, especially across the river. If you'll agree to see to my stock across the river when its cut off from the main ranch over here, I'll give you the ranch house and a hundred acres."

"For my own? To own myself?"

"Your own; that is, yours and Keewa's."

"Will I have to take care of the whole ranch across the river by myself?"

"Oh, no. There's no way you could do that by yourself. You, I, and the other hands will take care of that part of my ranch across the river. It'll be no different than the ranch on this side. You'll just have to do your best to keep the stock and the crops in good shape when I and the other hands are cut off. I expect you to take time to see to your own crops and stock also. I mean, I don't expect you to give up on your own interests and just see to mine. Just treat mine as good as you treat your own. That's all I ask."

"I'll do it, Mr. John, an' you woan ever be sorry."

"I know that, Sam. You're the only man I trust to look out for my interests."

"Does Miss Mary know 'bout this?"

"Not yet."

"I doan think she's gonna like it much, Mr. John."

"You may be right, Sam, but this is something that has to be if you're ever going to start your own family and I'm ever going to expand across the river. She really wants what's best for you. It's just that you are her only family from back East and she's afraid of losing you."

"There's no ways she can lose me Mista John."

"I know Sam, but I think she still a bit nervous and unsure of everything after what happened with Beth Magrath."

THE CHINOOK RIVER PRINCESS

John told Mary his plans at supper the next evening.
"I don't think I like that idea. Isn't it a bit soon?"
"It's the only way Sam will have a chance for a life of his own. If you love him you must let him go."
"I do love him. I like having him close."
"Across the river isn't too far."

Later, after John made sure the horses were bedded down properly in the barn and Mary finished the dishes, the two sat in the big room at the front of the house. Mary was crocheting a doily and John was working on reconciling his records of purchases with those of Mr. Kester.

John got up and retrieved his tobacco pouch and favorite pipe from its silk-lined box on the fireplace mantle. He affectionately rubbed the bowl of the pipe between his thumb and forefinger. It was the pipe Mary had given him. He packed the bowl with tobacco and was just putting a match to it, when Mary asked, "Did you hear something?"

"No. What did it sound like?"

"I think it's the horses. I think they're upset about something."

"It might be that mountain lion again. He keeps coming back. He probably still smells the afterbirth from that new foal." John placed his pipe back on the mantle. He quickly made his way across the room and picked up his Winchester which he always left on two pegs over the doorway.

Mary took the 44-40 off the gun rack to the right of the fireplace and followed him. When she got to the porch, John was half way to the barn. She kept the rifle barrel pointed in the air over John's head and the rifle butt just below her shoulder, so she could bring it into position and sight it quickly. There was a full moon so she could see clearly.

She saw John bring his rifle up and sight at something moving quickly from the back of the barn. He followed the fast-moving object with his sights but he didn't shoot. He walked back to the house.

"What was it?" Mary asked. "The mountain lion?"

"Yep, but I couldn't get a good shot and I don't want a wounded mountain lion roaming around the valley."

They both went in the house. John put his rifle back over the door and then went to the fireplace to get his pipe off the mantle once more. Mary reached high with the rifle to put it back on the rack. Just as John put the bowl of his pipe down in the pouch to load it with tobacco, the 44-40 went off. The explosion was deafening and the rifle jumped out of Mary's hands and hit the right wall. There was a deafening ringing in Mary's ears and through the cloud of smoke she saw John's mouth drop open as he back-pedaled across the room and slammed into the front wall, where he slid down into a sitting position.

"Oh my God, John, I've killed you!" Mary bolted across the room and knelt at John's feet. "I wasn't even touching the trigger. I didn't touch the trigger."

John put his hand on his chest and gasped for air. He looked down and searched for evidence of his wound, but there was none.

"You didn't hit me." His eyes were wide with wonder.

"What?" Mary yelled. "I can't hear you!"

John grabbed her by the upper arms and pulled her close and yelled in her left ear, "You missed me."

THE CHINOOK RIVER PRINCESS

"I missed you? I missed you? Oh my God!" she yelled at the ceiling, "I missed him!" Then she collapsed, sobbing in his arms.

"You pushed the barrel and made her miss," the dark angel whined. "He should be dead."
"You pulled the trigger. Did you think I wouldn't know?" The radiant angel shook her head disapprovingly.
"A minor point."

Epilogue

Mary died in bed at the age of eighty-two. She was surrounded by her three children, ten grandchildren, five great-grandchildren, and all of her many God and great-God children from the Grande Ranch across the river. She had led a full and happy life in the golden hills beside the Chinook River. She had outlived all of the men in her life and finally joined them in the small graveyard on the hill behind the house. She joined Sam, who had loved her as a daughter until he had his own, and John, who gave her life meaning, a home, and children she learned to love without the fear of losing. In spirit, she joined her mother, father, Jacob and little Josh.

In her final moments, she passed her father's gold ring on to her great grandson Samuel—a ring that, while in her possession, had recorded no lives taken, but one saved, that of Pawtuk. While Pawtuk always regretted saving Mary from the bear, it was that action which gave her the opportunity to save his life and thereby buoy the balance of Mankind's future just a bit.

Matt, who was sixty-two years old, stood with his fourteen year old grandson Samuel in the small graveyard behind the ranch house. Beside John March's tombstone, which read: born 1796 died 1860 was a new tombstone at the head of freshly filled grave. The new tombstone read: Mary Harper March - The Marches' Chinook River Princess- Born May 15, 1828 Passed July 7, 1910.

"So, you think great grandma lead a boring life stuck out here on the ranch?" Matt glanced sideways at his grandson.

"To hear mom tell it, all she did was cook, clean the house, knit, crochet, tat and sew."

Matt laughed. "Well, yes, she did all that. You have to remember, she lived most of her life in the olden days before trolley cars, the telephone, and electric lights, when the world was a boring place."

Samuel turned the snake ring around and around on his finger. "There isn't anything to do out here."

"You're right about that. This old ranch isn't anything like San Francisco." He Noticed Samuel turning the ring on his finger. "You shouldn't be wearing that ring for every day. Your great grandmother gave it to you as a family trust."

Samuel whined, "I know, grandad, I know. It was great-great grandpa Harper's ring... . I won't lose it. I promise.

"Why don't you go in and change out of those clothes. Your mother'll have my hide if you mess 'em up."

"Okay, grandad."

As Samuel walked back to the house, Matt looked up the hill to the tree line. He saw nothing and knitted his brow. Matt climbed the hillside, taking rests and catching his breath several times.

At the top of the hill, Matt found Pawtuk. The withered ancient warrior was resting in a heavily worn place on the dirt just outside the tree line.

Matt Squatted beside the body. "Oh, no, Pawtuk, not you too." Matt's eyes filled with tears as he gently stroked the thin long white hair on Pawtuk's head.

THE CHINOOK RIVER PRINCESS

Matt heard the characteristic whistle of a dove's wings beating the air and looked up in time to see a white dove alight in a small pine tree. He shrugged off a chill and apprehensively stroked the back of his neck. He turned, and coming toward him were three warriors on horseback. One was leading an extra mount. Matt stood and moved away from Pawtuk.

Ignoring Matt, the warriors dismounted, wrapped the body in a buffalo robe and laid it over the back of the extra horse. Then they mounted and rode at a slow walk back in the direction they had come, leading the horse bearing Pawtuk.

Matt walked back down the hillside toward the house. Behind him the small group of warriors rode very slowly over the crest of the hill in the opposite direction–behind them walked the Archangel.

Words from the author

I was inspired to write the Judgment Ring Books by a sermon given by Ray Chamberlain the minister of the Messiah United Methodist Church in West Springfield, Virginia. Since that time Mr. Chamberlain has moved on to other pastures and is now a bishop in Virginia. I have always missed him. The sermon Ray gave was based on the premise that there is no Recording Angel; no Angel who's job is to record all the sins of each man and woman and challenge each with their record on judgment day. Ray's sermons always had a meaningful and useful message, but in that sermon I missed it. I missed it because I quickly thought, "but what if there were something else; some inanimate object that did record the sins of mankind? What could it be and what exactly would it record and why?" From that hypothetical question the Judgment Ring was born.

I was further inspired to incorporate the westward movement in the first of my Judgment Ring Books during an inspection trip to a proposed hydroelectric dam site in Bliss, Idaho many years ago. I climbed from the Snake River up to the canyon rim at the edge of the town of Bliss with U.S.G.S. geologist Harold Malde. There he showed me a twenty-foot long slab of bedrock that had two parallel, six-inch deep cuts across it, about four feet apart. Harold asked if I knew what I was looking at and I said, "No idea." He smiled, "The Oregon Trail."

I was deeply moved by the thought of how many wagon wheels had crossed the very hard rock on their way west to have made such deep impressions.